SPACE & TIME

Spring/Summer 2024
Issue #146

PUBLISHER
Angela Yuriko Smith

PUBLISHER · AUDIO VISUAL PRODUCER
Ryan Aussie Smith

EDITOR-IN-CHIEF
Angela Yuriko Smith

FICTION EDITOR
Gerard Houarner

POETRY EDITOR
Linda D. Addison

ART EDITOR
Diane Weinstein

FOREIGN SUBMISSIONS EDITOR
Luiz F. Peters

EDITORS EMERITUS
Gordon Linzner
Hildy Silverman
Austin Gragg

FEATURE WRITERS
Linda D. Addison
Daniel M. Kimmel
Briant Laslo
Michael Wyatt

EDITORIAL ASSISTANT
Kyra Starr
Ken Hueler

FIRST READERS
Querus Abuttu
Susan Hanniford Crowley
Kathleen David
Gary Frank
Melissa French
Dan Keithan
Edward Greaves
Faith Justice
Felicia Martinez
Jennifer M. Perrson
Rhonda Schlumpberger
Samuel D. Stinson
Lee Weinstein

ARTWORK
Alan F. Beck
Doug Draper
Alfred Klosterman
Arthur Haywood
Prettysleepy Art
Anthony R. Rhodes
Al Sirois
Angela Yuriko Smith

COVER ART
Matthew Schuler

LAYOUT DESIGN
Anthony R. Rhodes

PROOF READER
Allen Thobois

In Memoriam: Matthew Schuler Claire Fitzpatrick	1
Chantico Lee Clark Zumpe	2
Goodbye Mother Donna J. W. Munro	3
Transhuman Evolution Robin Helweg-Larsen	7
Lost Ark F. J. Bergmann	7
DAATH Jose Ángel Conde	9
Diffusion Brian U. Garrison	15
I heard the little girl got caught in the big M. C. Childs	15
Take Two On The Movies - Notes on "The Invisible Man" Daniel M. Kimmel	16
JUST, LIKE, DON'T Dom Gerard	21
Grandi Successi Edoardo Maroncelli	23
Plague Hag KT Wagner	26
The Ring of Destiny Michael H. Payne	29
Magic Mushroom Sam Crain	39
Blood and Space C. H. Williams	43
This is What I Am (I Sing of Revolution) Felicia Martínez	44
The Shepherd's Enantiodromia J. S. Graham	45
At the Edge of the World, There Were No Gods Maxwell I. Gold	45
The Troll Michael Bacchia	46
Solar System Real Estate Casey Aimer	46
Her Father's Daughter Spencer Sekulin	47
I Wish...I Wish You'd Be Happy Jeffrey Ogochukwu	62
After the War Jonathan Ukah	63
Fusion Friends and the Purple Cow Craig Brownlie	65
ZODGILLA Kurt Newton	69
The Definitive, Indisputable, All Time Top 7 (my favorite) Summer-time Horror Movies Ever Released Briant Laslo	72
All The Dazz Don DeBrandt	75
Never the Netherwood C. H. Lindsay	83
Word Ninja Linda D. Addison	85
The Mx. Up: Transmissions from Beyond the Binary Writer's Log: 004A Michael Wyatt	86

On Radical Kindness, or How $5 Bought Me New Life

From the Editor's Desk

In my late teens, I was homeless. I hitchhiked, slept in concrete doorways and mostly starved. This was in Boulder, Colorado in the late 80s and there were quite a few of us runaway, homeless kids. Some of us were fleeing abuse. Others had been kicked out. We were all afraid.

We reacted to the fear in different ways. We shaved our heads and acted mean so people would leave us alone—strike before struck. We hurled insults at strangers to harden our own bruised hearts. We tried to mask our fear with whatever we could find: alcohol, drugs, whippets, sex. As far as members of society go, we were pretty unpleasant by most standards.

After a few years of this, I wound up pregnant. To me, this was a message from the universe to clean up my act and be a mother, which also meant I needed to start eating, and that was a problem. Desperate, one night, I traded the only treasure I had left to a worker at a Dunkin' Donuts in exchange for a sandwich. He said I could get it back if I had $5 by the end of his shift. I went down to Pearl Street Mall to beg. I had two hours.

I should have been able to scrape up that amount in half the time, but that night I couldn't get a penny. As my payment deadline neared, I came to grips with the reality that I was probably going to lose my bracelet, a gift from a friend. I headed back to see if I could make another deal.

On the way, I stopped outside a grocery store about to close. There was hardly anyone there, but I made a final attempt. A man exited, clutching his grocery bags and hurrying to his car.

"Excuse me, sir?" I started, and then I trailed off. It was cold and he had hurried on out of earshot.

What was the point? In my mind, I'd reached the end. I was going to lose the bracelet. I was most likely going to lose the baby I had just begun to accept as reality. I was always losing things. That's how one becomes a loser.

The man stopped, and turned to look at me. "Did you say something?"

"Oh, I was just going to ask if you had any spare change… but it doesn't matter."

He walked toward me, reached into his pocket and pulled out a $5 bill. He pressed it into my hand. "It *does* matter," he said. "And so do you. Don't ever forget that."

And then he was gone. I went back to the Dunkin' Donuts with five minutes to spare, got my bracelet, which I probably lost soon after, and went on with my life. One thing I've never lost was the message paired with, for me, a radical act of kindness.

Now it's 2024, and I've just begun to read Octavia E. Butler's *Parable of the Sower*. While written in 1993, the story begins in 2024, now, when Butler's fictional United States has grown unstable due to climate change, growing wealth inequality, and corporate greed. *Wait… is this fiction or fortune telling?*

At this moment, there are a shocking amount of human beings in the world standing in the dark, hungry and alone. Some of us need actual food. Others are starving for connection. Many, many of us are afraid. We all show our fear in different ways.

We might leave angry comments on social media and act mean so people will leave us alone—strike before struck. We hurl insults at strangers to harden our own bruised hearts. We try to mask our fear with whatever we can find: alcohol, drugs, whipped cream, sex. As far as members of society go, we can all be pretty unpleasant by some standards.

I've changed a lot since I was that starving waif in Colorado, but I can still find myself standing alone in the dark sometimes, thinking I have nowhere else to go. At those times, I think back to that radical act of kindness that has held so much more value to me than a truckload of $5 bills.

Wherever he is, I hope he has been blessed a thousandfold. Wherever you are, if you need an inoculation of self-worth, share mine, gifted from a stranger. And no matter how dark things get, may we never forget that a small act of kindness can change a world.

"It *does* matter, and so do you. Don't ever forget that."

"When you really know somebody, you can't hate them. Or maybe it's just that you can't really know them until you stop hating them." Orson Scott Card, in *Speaker for the Dead*

Angela Yuriko Smith
Publisher/Editor-in-Chief

THE OLDEST CONTINUOUSLY PUBLISHED SPECULATIVE FICTION SEMI-PRO MAGAZINE IN PRINT
PUBLISHED SINCE 1966

Fall/Winter 2023

In Memoriam: Matthew Schuler
By Claire Fitzpatrick

My husband, Matthew Schuler (1988-2024) was an amazing artist, though he kept to himself, and many of his friends didn't even know about his talent. While he had always been artistic, played guitar, and composed music, he didn't start painting until 2019.

Though he experimented with different mediums, one day, he came across an artist painting with spray paint. He watched a few videos of the artist, the methods he employed, and then one day, he said to me, 'I can do that.' So, he learned, and he painted almost every day. Within a few months, he had almost two dozen paintings.

His favourite thing to paint were planets. He loved space, science fiction, and the idea of the unknown. It's no surprise his favourite author was HP Lovecraft. Over time, as his painting improved, I suggested he submit a few of his favourites to speculative fiction magazines. He was hesitant, unsure, and told me not to. But what did I do? I contacted them anyway. *New Myths Magazine* featured his piece 'Incoming Star Spawn' in Issue 52, September 15, 2020. *AntipodeanSF* featured his piece 'Black Hole (Blue)' in Issue 261, June 2020. Many of his friends bought paintings from him. A shop even displayed three of them in their lobby. Though he'd never say it, Matt was proud of his achievements.

We bought our house in 2020 and planned to build a studio for him. He was excited while looking at houses and had specific requirements for his studio. Not too much shade, not too much sun, out of the wind. While planning, we set up a smaller area for him to paint. He bought paint and materials and started looking at his colour wheel for ideas. And then, in December 2020, his mental health declined, he told me to stop contacting magazines, and he stopped painting altogether.

This January, Matt took his own life. I cannot begin to describe the emptiness I feel within my heart. A creative, wonderful spirit is gone. I discovered his body, and while I try to block the image from my mind, it's still there. I am saddened he will never paint again, for it brought him so much joy. But I will endeavour to share his art with as many people as I can.

Ever mine, ever thine, ever ours.

Claire Fitzpatrick is a Shadows award-winning, Ditmar nominated, and Bram Stoker shortlisted speculative fiction and non-fiction author. President and social media coordinator of the Australasian Horror Writers Association. Readers can find more of Matthew's artwork on his website: https://miseryinkdesign.blog

Chantico
Lee Clark Zumpe

I see her there, sitting hearthside,
a crown of cactus spikes and red snakes
perched on her head, brooding,
her eyes downcast in wistfulness,
entranced by the fire's glowing embers —
each glowing cinder reminiscent
of Popocatépetl's lake of molten rock.

I see her there, sitting on a folding chair,
haggling with locals and tourists
at the Mercado de Xochimilco,
her face an ancient, half-forgotten dream,
her smile as bright and beautiful
as the sun breaking through storm clouds.

Goodbye Mother

Written by Donna J. W. Munro
Illustrated by Al Sirois

There were warnings.

I guess I saw them first, but they were there for anyone paying attention.

Rising seas. Warming by degrees a year. Fires. Floods. Plagues.

Mother earth had withdrawn her protections.

I took a drag off a cigarette, letting the sweet smoke linger in my mouth before sucking it down into my lungs. Fire in space is a terrible waste of resources and such a huge risk, but what was the point of being a gazillionaire if you couldn't buy a last second of happiness?

The computer started to alert me, *"Mr. Trask—"*

"What did I tell you, Lixa?"

"Captain Trask. I apologize. Shall I run the system checks?"

"Please… Just quietly, okay?"

"Yes, Captain. Turning level to five. External checks, running. Hull integrity, satisfactory. Solar sail, operational. Light cells, full…"

I stood and stretched, then stubbed my cigarette out into the ashtray. The litany of scans didn't matter to me. They'd come back perfect. My engineers were all at least as brilliant as me. They'd all earned their places in the belly of the ARC— my swan song.

Atmosphere Runner Cryo-galleon.

"Human pods at 100%. All internal diagnostics on our guests are stable and holding…"

Coffee. A final coffee and one more cigarette. That's what the doctor ordered.

The ARC had taken all my profits from the cars, the planes, the computers and software, the investments in internet start ups, but I didn't care.

Money wasn't the currency of the future.

I'd made the ARC perfect and hand-picked the specimens now filling the belly of the hold. The brightest and best. The strongest. The ones I knew would make a better world when we landed. Doctors and teachers and poets and artists.

But none like me.

"Animal containment pods at 100%. Seeds and plant cuttings at optimal temperature."

The ship had no pilot. No crew. Just a smart operating system with directives so clear and simple, I knew they'd never fail.

1. Protect the pods and their inhabitants over all else.

2. Monitor the earth for stability.

3. Bring the pod back to earth when it was safe to inhabit.

The subroutines surrounding those directives had taken me years to write. I'd considered every need, every angle, every defining bit of code and then my program gurus combed the lovely construct I'd made. When they declared it genius, I'd named her Lixa and had given a downgraded version called AL-Lixa out to the masses to use withtheir phones and homes to

Space and Time

do little tasks. Through AL-Lixa, I'd searched out my "guests." Clever algorithms weeded out the assholes. The smallest number needed to sustain a genetically viable human group has been set at one hundred and sixty, but I'd found that number to be inadequate. Skilled people had demands. They wanted to save their husbands and wives. Their children. They knew getting on the ARC meant leaving everything and there were just some things they wouldn't leave. Besides, I like redundancy in a system.

Imagine a town with one plumber and that one plumber died one morning. The learning curve for the rest of the town to figure out who next should plumb might leave them hip deep in shit and dying from cholera. Consider the problems of no one knowing how to build or farm or heal because there's only one.

I settled on a cross section of five thousand of every background I could find.

Plus, the animals.

Plus, the seeds and water purifiers and tools and machines.

And the books—some paper, some electronic. I had librarians put together a wonderful cross section of reading, but you've never seen so much pain as when you ask a librarian to reject millions of books for damaging influences and dangerous ideas. In the end, they couldn't come to an agreement.

Instead, I designed an algorithm. It completed the task by reading every review ever written and cross referencing the academic uses of the literature or work while screening for and eliminating certain words and toxic ideas.

Tom Sawyer didn't make it.

Neither did the works of James Baldwin, for the exact same reason. A shame, that one. Great writer.

And for some reason, none of the religious texts made it.

I don't argue with algorithms though.

It's been up here a week, skimming the upper atmosphere in an eternally correcting orbit. When I was making all those electric planes and cars, I was really practicing to build this.

A thing of beauty, my ARC.

I pulled up my captain's chair next to the only window in the whole ship.

My room.

Out the window, I watched those poor bastards on earth playing out their Shakespearian tragedy. We'd been on the verge of this war for one hundred years, but in the last twenty, the Russians and their dictator for life had stoked hate across the globe. Our presidents were picked by idiots, brainwashed by North Korean and Chinese meme artists, skilled at wearing away humanity and stoking patriot idiocy.

I sipped my coffee and lit my last smoke, savoring the flavor of it. Such nasty flavors. Acquired tastes really.

Tobacco and coffee hadn't made it into the memory banks and I hope the adults, all non-smokers and reeducated to understand the importance of their words and their teachings, let the wild versions stay in the deep woods that will grow up in the scars and scorch marks of the war.

Through my window, the curve of the earth lit up with another volley of flashing mushrooms. This time, India and southeast Asia.

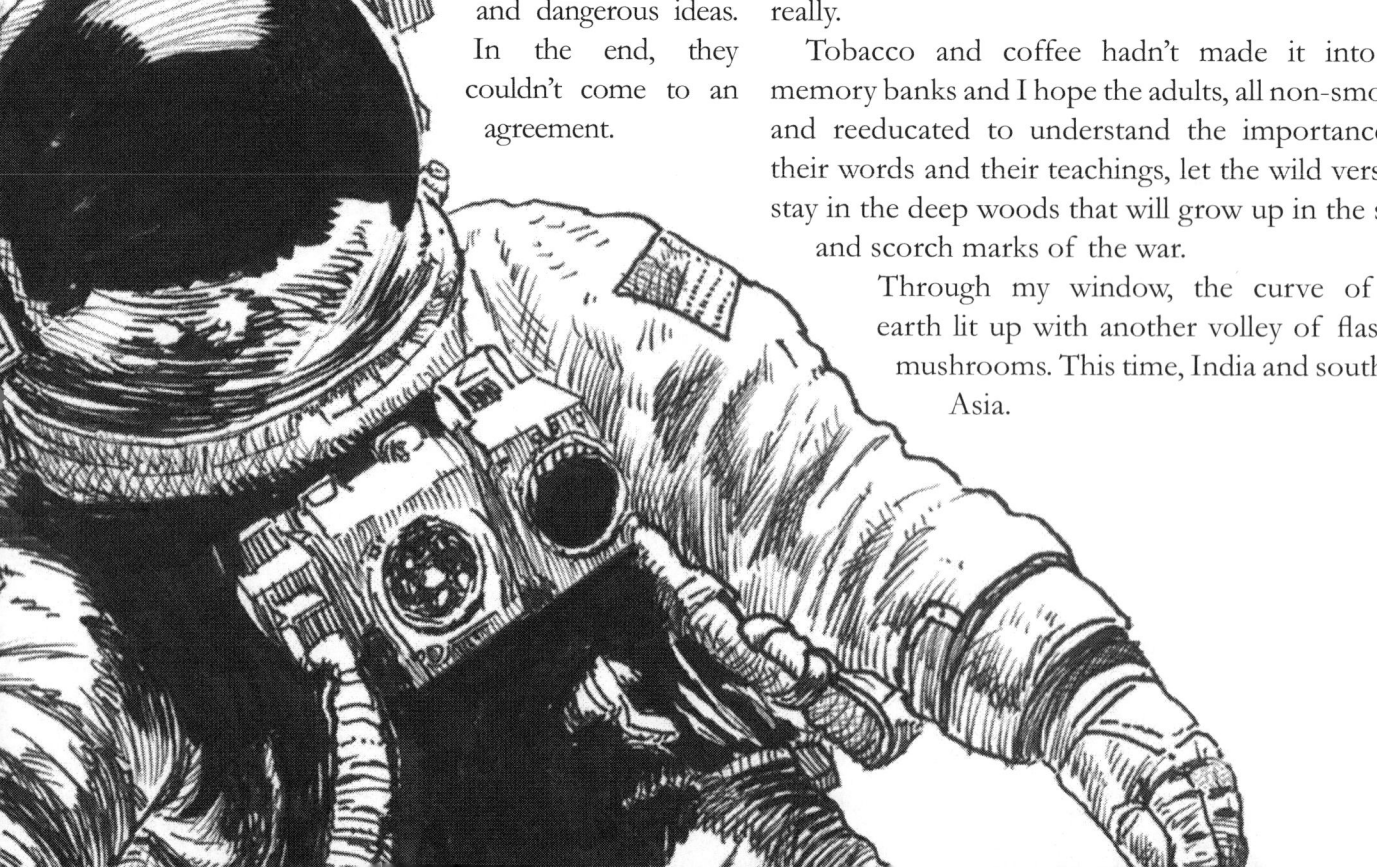

I glanced over at the read out. Over one hundred nuclear bomb blasts since we lifted off the week before. Alongside those blasts, volcanoes erupted and spewed thick ash clouds into theatmosphere below us in cloudy, poisonous streams.

"Captain, the scans suggest that the tipping point has passed. The blasts you see now are reflex launches set off by the firestorms and the launch platform's own protective programming."

That's it then.

"Lixa, give me another five minutes, huh? I'll finish my coffee and my smoke, then we can begin."

"Yes, Captain."

"Based on your estimates, how long before the earth is inhabitable again?" I asked her.

She was silent for a long moment, then, *"At least a thousand years. It is within the ship's capacity to last five times longer though."*

I smiled. She was trying to make me feel better. A damned program had more heart than most of humanity had. Well, used to have.

I took another deep drag, loving how the cigarette burned my lungs, then blew the smoke out. It swirled around my head like the hurricanes below that dotted the face of the earth.

Man, was Mother pissed.

"Captain?"

One more puff and a sip of my cooled coffee.

"It's a shame I won't get to see it, Lixa...what they do with a fresh start."

"Yes. But you understand the algorithm's decision."

"I wrote it to make hard choices, Lixa. I'm exactly the kind of person who caused this bullshit. Venture capitalists. Racists. Weak minded dumbasses. Politicians and lawyers. All the destruction and the bullheadedness. Profit margins and resource management. Fucking Manifest Destiny. They don't need any of that. Besides, I don't argue with algorithms."

"Shall I release you?"

I nodded and pulled on the helmet that would give me a few extra seconds.

The gravity in the room went first and drops of brown coffee broke from the mass in the cup and floated in orbs that shimmied and stretched.

Then the oxygen drained away. My cigarette's bright red cherry winked out.

Finally, the pop and hiss of the airlock door as it opened.

Space is cold, but the atmosphere isn't.

I didn't have time to freeze when I fell below ARC's skimming orbit.

I burned as gravity pulled me home.

Before my helmet failed and my eyes boiled, I had the greatest view a human has ever seen. Just me and the horizon from so far up the whole world looked like an eye watching me.

Before I shredded in the friction of the atmosphere, I recited my epitaph.

"Goodbye, Mother."

Donna J. W. Munro's pieces are published in *Nothing's Sacred Magazine* IV and V, *Corvid Queen, Hazard Yet Forward, Enter the Apocalypse, Beautiful Lies/Painful Truths II, Terror Politico, It Calls from the Forest, Gray Sisters Vol 1, Pseudopod 752, Shakespeare Unleashed,* and others. Check out her novel, *Revelation: Poppet Cycle Book 1*. Contact her at https://www.donnajwmunro.com or @DonnaJWMunro on Twitter.

AVAILABLE NOW

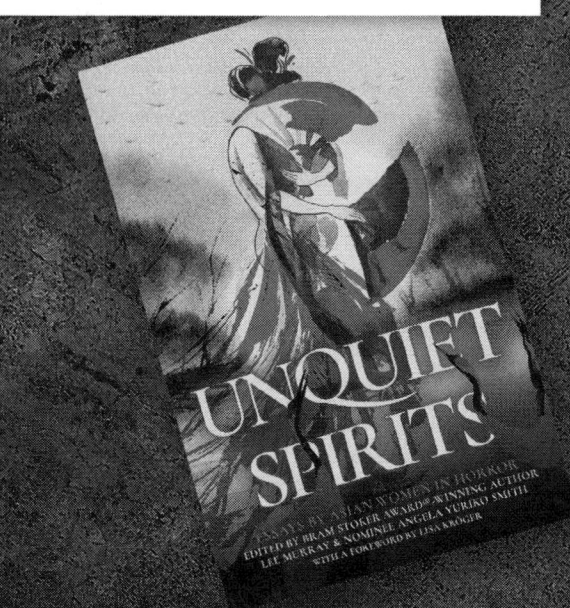

"A powerhouse of cultural revelation."
—Midwest Book Review

"The spirits don't whisper in this collection, they roar across the pages."
—Horror Addicts

"A deeply emotional and insightful exploration of the female Asian experience by some of the best writing talent today."
—Tosca Lee, New York Times bestselling author

"A tight view on the symbolism of the monstrous feminine... struck a deep chord."
—Interzone Magazine

CHECK OUT OUR FULL CATALOG OF TITLES FROM WOMEN IN HORROR

@BlackSpotBooks
www.BlackSpotBooks.com

Transhuman Evolution
Robin Helweg-Larsen

The humans crowd the riverbanks in cities
while you, would-be transhuman in your boat,
trust to your dreams and luck as on you float,
ignoring all the land's static committees,
the buildings taller with their strident voices,
the citied banks ever more crammed and loud,
leaders and statues oversize and proud,
fixed in their views. But you see other choices.

And then there's no more land. Only the sea.
You deso-, iso-, yet e-lated find
after the Desolation of the Years,
sailing and searching past humanity
in the vast oceans of the future mind,
a life within the music of the spheres.

Lost Ark
F. J. Bergmann

Once Noah realized that the gross estimate
was off by at least one standard deviation,
recalculations showed that a second vessel
was required. The extraordinary nature
of the problem called for a bold solution.
Some ideologies were not comfortable
in close proximity, and they had never felt
at ease with certain minorities anyway.
They were relieved when the other ship
drifted off into its darkening mysteries
with a blindfolded basilisk at the helm,
dragon wings spread like immense sails,
the unicorn as bowsprit, Saint Elmo's fire
dancing on the dazzle of its twisted horn.

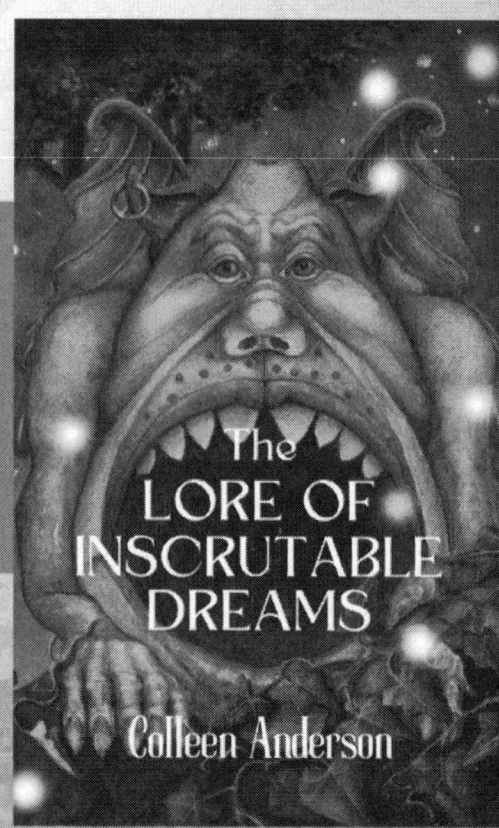

The LORE OF INSCRUTABLE DREAMS

Colleen Anderson

Available now!!! *The Lore of Inscrutable Dreams* by Colleen Anderson; a speculative poetry journey into the depths of the human experience, exploring themes of female empowerment, forging one's own path, and the power of fairytales and magic within us. A masterful blend of imagination, symbolism, and emotion, with an introduction by award-winning author Linda D. Addison.

From yurikopublishing.com

Yuriko Publishing

DAATH

Written by Jose Ángel Conde
Illustrated by Angela Yuriko Smith

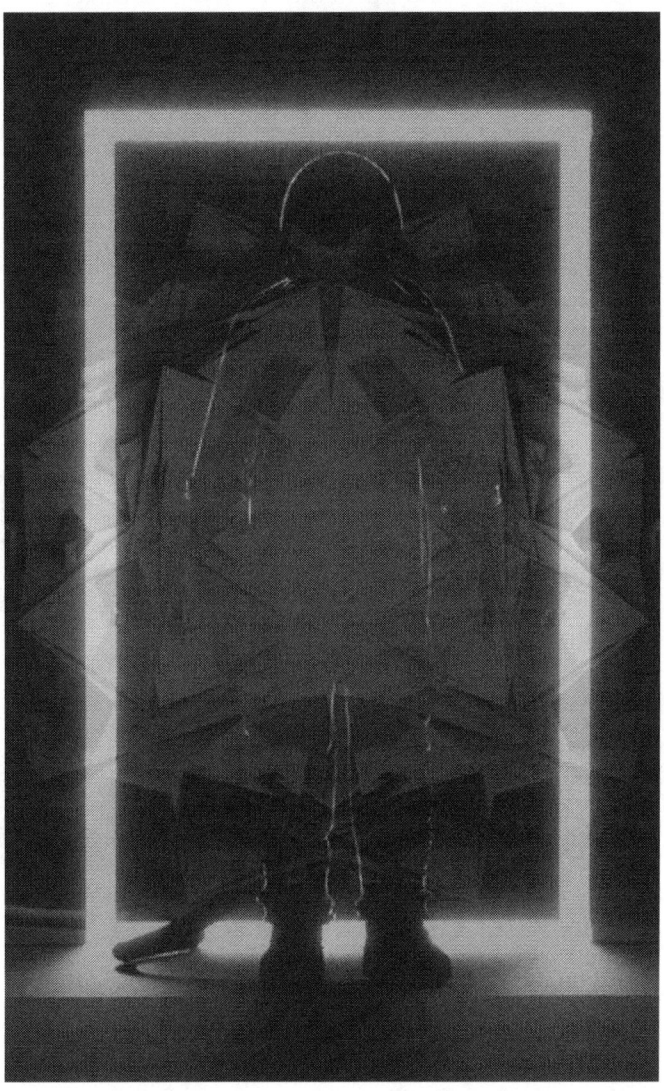

BRAIN 4

The door to the fourth dimension is already here thanks to BRAIN 4.

A revolutionary surgical procedure that will turn you into a true metahuman.

By mimicking the geometric expansion process of the octagon, our surgeons manage to expand the capacity of our, until now, limited brain to allow it to accommodate two additional, virtual but fully operational brain hemispheres. The resulting four hemispheres are compressed into a single ectoplasmic space during everyday life and will only expand after a brief session of strategically applied reflexology to your pineal gland. All for a modest monthly fee!

Both the subsequent physical alterations and the fourfold increase in the usual size of the cranial mass have been extensively tested and are the result of decades of study on the anatomy of civilizations like those inhabiting Alpha Reticuli and Aldebaran. Space-time travel and contact with other entities are finally within your reach!

BRAIN 4
A product of Tetra Inc.

"Extraterrestrial entities?"

Jesse Kuunainen understands that Saul's question is the beginning of a new session of reproaches and mockery about his work. It was always like this, but he was the only person he could trust. So, he decides it's best to cut to the chase and clearly present his findings. Jesse stops the demonstration video and turns off the micro-computer chip so that his explanations capture all the attention.

"I am aware that so far, expeditions beyond the Solar System have only found corpses, and their autopsies have not been able to satisfactorily reproduce their brain activity pattern. Still, you know as well as I do that the latest theories regarding their anatomical constitution point to brains with four hemispheres."

"You said it yourself: 'theories,'" Saul says. "I understand that your youthful enthusiasm may be awakened by the extraterrestrial hypothesis, but the multi-billion-dollar donations from trans-earthly companies are not invested in speculation. For a commercial video targeting a lay audience, it might be a good hook, but we are working at the highest level of scientific research. Furthermore, there are rumors that the Chinese and Russian stations on the far side of the Moon keep presenting new projects every week in almost all their research fields. You know very well that we cannot waste time on this, Jesse."

Jesse's icy figure remains motionless against the backdrop of the lunar surface, which the distance blurs into a sea of soft milky appearance, framing the snow of his gray eyes, his indigo-tinted fringe with his ethereal skin, almost transparent under his pale mauve blouse. His immobility is due both to his usual melancholic posture and to a reassessment of strategy. Then he decides to take out the crystal octagon from his backpack and place it on the aluminum table.

Saul watches it without knowing what to say, just examining its structure. It is a symmetrical object barely five centimeters in wingspan, with an octagonal shape repeated in new replicas of the outer face concentrically and decreasing towards the inside, leaving similar spaces between each ring of eight faces, like a spiral.

The reverse side is completely flat, as if it served as a base. Saul leans over the table to get a better look, and a final glimpse reveals the geometric figure within the tiny center of the innermost octagonal section: a circle inserted into an equilateral triangle from which three crossed lines radiate, forming a star, with their intersections giving rise to a total of seven points.

"A Fano plane?" Saul drags the words, emitting a reverberation of disbelief. "What does all this mean? A project of projective geometry?"

"Holograms. I'm using the mathematics of octonion numbers to manipulate the electromagnetic dimension of the reflected light from the optic nerve that impacts the pineal gland, thus expanding brain perception. This octagon is just a sample."

In reality, the system would consist of two parts, emitter and receiver. The first octagon, the emitter, the size of a microchip, would be inserted into the pineal gland, following the scheme of the Fano plane to reproduce with laser beams one-eighth of colors that make up the known space-time: red, green, blue, cyan, magenta, yellow, and the black that will form in the center after creating a toroidal light field. The subject with the implant stands in the center of a second Fano plane on a macro scale, inserted into a second large octagon, like in a pool with mirrored walls. In synchronized fashion, the two devices, micro and macro, would begin to rotate following the principle of particle accelerators but in opposite directions: the first octagon counterclockwise and inverted, following the "camera obscura" principle, and the second one specularly in a clockwise direction.

The combined kinetics of both light spectra created by the two toroidal fields would expand perception and make visible the threshold of strings, the boundary at which hyperspace would begin to manifest.

"Jesse, give me a minute, please. What you're saying could be plausible but... look, really... I will never doubt that you are a very brilliant woman. The problem is that perhaps you are not being too realistic, and..."

For a moment, Jesse notices a slight tremor in Saul's hand as he wipes away sudden drops of sweat on his forehead. Her bewilderment increases when her partner nervously looks around before addressing her again.

"Where would we get the resources for such a project? Who would allow us to develop it? It's better not to investigate these things. I think the artificial gravity of the colony is affecting you." He gets up as if his seat were red-hot, startling Jesse. "I need to go to the restroom."

"What if I've already started testing it?"

"Don't be crazy..." Saul's trembling fingers struggle to fasten his already open jacket.

Jesse Kuunainen doesn't take her eyes off her partner until he disappears down the hallway leading to the restrooms. When she turns her eyes back to the lunch table, it seems that the other patrons are collectively averting their gaze from her. She pauses for a moment and then runs her fingers between her brows, massaging her skin with them. The pressure of the domes of the European lunar station. It's a miracle that there is a budget to provide them with oxygen while hunger riots continue on Earth. On the Moon, scientists like her stage a new cold war for technological progress. Two different worlds in a spiral that were destined to collide, no matter how many light-years they put between them.

Jesse tries to focus on eating and reaches for the foam wrapper of the burger. The slogan on the lid greets her like a mocking oracle against a lilac background: "Thanatos. A burger of death." When she opens it and smells the fried beef, a wave of nausea confirms that she'd rather look at the lunar landscape through the front window. Sometimes she thinks she would feel better out there alone, accompanied only by the cold.

The dark vision of the space sky soothes her eyes as if they were closed. But the screen of nothingness is relaxing only for a few moments because it always ends up projecting images on it. A ring of cooked meat fragments begins to rotate where the stars should be, drawing Jesse's attention back inside the diner, towards the column of hamburger pieces forming a miniature tornado in front of her, reaching up to the ceiling, with its epicenter in the foam container. Changing its speed, the meat pieces descend slowly to converge into a spinning disk, resembling a toroid, with a hollow center in which four letters in an unknown language shine. Jesse leans slightly, breaking out of her paralysis, and before she can read them, a flash blinds the scene, transporting an infinite voice:

"Fundament."

The plasma ship falls through dimensions, heading towards the rotating traction field of the spiral, whose particles form the arms of a galaxy shaped like a space starfish. The metaxynaut's body is fused with the material and the evolutions of the bolide they pilot, so that the combined kinetics of both, pilot and vehicle, gives them an immaterial quality with which to navigate through various planes of existence.

The pilot's head is inserted into the octonion cube, its algorithms gleaming along its surface like hieroglyphs of interdimensional code, marking the course to follow. Coordinates are dictated by the giant entity serving as a copilot, its slender and fibrous body composed of silver lights arranged to mimic humanoid anatomy. Navigation numbers are not transmitted through sounds but appear as luminescent blocks at the bottom of its featureless face, amidst what appear to be two vaginal lips of plasma framing a word-emitting tunnel. Mathematics reaches the metaxynaut's mind through synaptic electrical currents. Suddenly, the communication flow is interrupted.

"Ilet."

The ship assumes a vertical position in weightless space-time and is parallelly attracted to a celestial body that fills that part of the sky with its shape resembling a spinal cord or a writhing, vertebrate serpent, covering the cosmos. The bolide is tethered to the photons of this galactic column, and after a brief interval, it begins to descend slowly towards the spiral, embraced at a distance by its orbit. In the hollow of the entity inside the ship and the vertex of the galaxy outside, it seems as if a single white mouth is forming, speaking simultaneously from both poles, in the vortices of their brilliance.

"Eht larbetrev nmuloc fo eht caidoz, gniyrrac eth sluos fo snamuh ni eth mrof fo segassem. S'taht tahw ouy llac eth "reitnorf", tub rof eth Renni Eripme, ereht era no seiradnuob."

Jesse Kuunainen walks on the surface of Mare Australe, the infinite expanse of craters that stretches from the visible face to the far side of the Moon. Kuunainen, "the Moon woman" in her native Finnish, the country where a woman with her genius is considered insane and now only remembered as the vessel where lakes settled to reflect the silent and unflinching Earth's satellite. The moment closes like a mirror, the Moon and Earth occupying their respective places in the firmament simultaneously.

Suddenly, Jesse notices that she is naked, but the absence of a spacesuit does not seem deadly, as if she were in an intermediate space, neither lunar nor terrestrial, where its own atmosphere prevails. However, the cold is real, as are the white grains of soil that rise from the sea of craters, caressing her skin like lunar butterflies. Jesse closes her eyes in fear when the particles reach her cheeks, but after a while, she opens them again, comfortable with the soft touch they produce.

Now the sky appears without stars, and the white grains rush to paint on the empty canvas of space's blackness, making her hair fly until it hangs from the zodiac. Lines of words from alphabets she does not know begin to form around her life, suspended in space and perhaps in time, like threads of thought playing at weaving the universe, solidifying into stars. Among the celestial filaments emerges a featureless face at its center, which begins to rotate with wisdom, first taking the form of a circle within a triangle, and then bending inward infinitely in a spiral, like an interstellar gate opening or luminous jaws folding. The floating words, visible and audible, are like a stellar breath:

"Ilet."

Space and Time

Iósif Beliónov tightly grips his Dragunov rifle as rings formed by strange luminous letters appear, crackling like fire in the night air. Seconds before, the few reindeer that were treading the snowy and silent tundra had frenziedly fled towards the uncertain shelter of distant groups of trees, alerting the muscles of the albino soldier who was waiting, hidden, lying under his camouflage blanket. Beliónov had come to this area just a few kilometers from Finland, western territory, on a special mission for the Svarog division, a unit of the KGB created to investigate the growing wave of UFO cases.

"It is written that the tzadikim, the "Righteous," will come from the planet Bilón to wage the battle for human souls and will enter through messages written with the words contained in the Sephiroth of the Tree of Life - the rabbi of the northernmost synagogue in the Soviet Union had told him. The religious man never removed his body from the straps and cubes of his tefilim since he first saw the phenomena, which he claimed occurred every winter night for a month now. - It will be the beginning of the ultimate Exodus, the Dimensional Exodus."

Beliónov's grayish eyes try to discern the floating letters, in what appears to be an impossible mixture of Cyrillic and Hebrew. His mood changes to astonishment when, suddenly, the alphabetical rings merge into a single word that takes him back to his Jewish origins:

קשר

"Qesher," "connection."

An impulse, born more from an uncontrollable subconscious atavism than from courage, urges him to get up from the snowy ground and head decisively towards the fiery seal, rifle at the ready. A blinding circle of light is then projected onto the wasteland for several meters, imprisoning Beliónov in its center. Paralyzed, his body begins to rise in the air, drawn in the direction of a cylindrical beam of light that disappears into the sky.

The prismatic eyes of Beliónov seek the origin of the reverse gravity field until, floating above it, Beliónov can observe a large object with a surface resembling that of an elongated rock. In the center of its visible face, a symbol shines, formed by a circle in the center of an equilateral triangle that gradually contracts its vertices inward, like concave petals forming an opening to a stroboscopic interior.

The intermittent flashes pull Jesse out of her lethargy, forcing her to open her eyes. The sample octagon is still on the aluminum table, but now its center emits a flickering light. Everything she observes seems to be filtered through a transparent layer that moves in waves, as if the air had condensed into a substance that is between liquid and ectoplasmic. She can even perceive the waves coming from the silent air conditioning system, vibrating as if they were hitting an invisible barrier that prevents their passage.

In this new atmosphere, micro-organisms or plankton, which seem to have exponentially increased in size, float around, as she imagines them. Jesse gets up, and after a few seconds of disorientation, her vision seems to begin to define the objects she sees in this state, so alien that the neuroscientist begins to doubt with which organs of her anatomy she is perceiving it. Between clumsiness and terror, she grabs the octagon with what she believes is in her hand and starts moving through Thanatos Burger.

At her first step, Jesse feels like she's about to stumble, but she passes through the tables, which under normal conditions should have been an obstacle, without her sense of touch being altered, except for a slight, moist pulsation that occurs somewhere on her.

She tries to rationalize what is happening and feels a kind of reflex recognition leading her thoughts to elaborate the theory of an amniotic world or, venturing even further into her conjectures and equivalences, a cellular landscape. It seems that with this self-conviction, her supposed walking improves, but the next thing she finds in her path is much more difficult and terrifying to process.

In the field of vision now open before Jesse, Saul appears with a huge leech-like creature attached to his back, a massive leech the size of a man, with its large suction mouth inserted up to Saul's lips.

The suction noises are deafening and occur with each relentless contraction of the parasite, culminating in a process that causes an extraordinary and repulsive reaction developed in several sinister stages: first, all of Saul's blood exits his body in the form of an exact replica of himself, but composed of hemoglobin, with his corresponding head, body, and blood limbs; next, a second body composed of his internal organs separates from Saul, followed by a third body corresponding to his skeleton, and finally, a fourth body made of flesh and skin.

While the different separated bodies float parallel through space, one behind the other, advancing towards Jesse, it seems that the only thing left alive of Saul is a bright plasma that wriggles at the bottom of the dissections like a worm, grasped by the giant leech's suckers.

Jesse's panic is articulated in a shudder that makes her discover that the same process is repeating with all the customers in the restaurant and with the inhabitants of the colony that she manages to see beyond the threshold of the fast-food establishment. In those brief seconds of distraction, Saul's blood body impacts against her, disintegrating and staining her skin with several liters of red liquid. Then, the parasites straighten up in unison and look at her like a spring, a single mind ready to attack. Jesse grips the octagon with all her strength.

Jesse Kuunainen's being now advances through a network of translucent tunnels that extends across the entire surface of the lunar colony, like an intestine or the inside of a crystalline caterpillar, crossing the kilometers in which the spaces of the installation are structured in seconds. They are nodes that fold space, and she only has to walk with her mind to form and cross them. In just a few minutes, Jesse emerges in a space closed by a dome of the same immaterial matter. She stops in the center of the room to confirm that she has reached the area of the vast hangar serving as a port for the massive translunar cruisers. The interdimensional dome that surrounds her begins to solidify into increasingly fleshy matter, appearing to engulf the boarding area. Jesse now distinguishes two giants closing what seems like a rift at the only open end of the enveloping fabric.

They are two beings with elongated heads, whose faces seem like half of a face inserted in the collision of two mirrors, resulting in the symmetric reflections of a deformed anatomy. A new dome emerges and folds inward into the covering skin in the process of solidification, forming inside it a gigantic transparent sphere that strives to be shot upward, like a ganglion or an astral tumor. The immense ectoplasmic balloon manages to pierce the fabric of the tissue and exits into space with Jesse inside, the lunar cold bristling her pale limbs.

The sphere now takes the form of one of the emergency escape pods, through whose window she can see the entire lunar colony exploding in a massive white nuclear mushroom. The shockwave shakes the module, which rises until the view of the moon's globe is lost. Jesse floats weightlessly through the cabin in time to enter one of the available spacesuits.

A quick check allows her to discover with the subsequent amazement that she is actually inside the experimental capsule detached from a Russian-made Photon-type research satellite. Overcoming the Cyrillic characters barrier, her theoretical knowledge of this and other spacecraft allows her to conclude that the ship's oxygen is depleted, and its navigation system is damaged. Communications are also not working.

Jesse lets herself float in zero gravity as if it were an act of acceptance. Hours may pass before she sees a purple foam container pass in front of her helmet visor, reading, "A Death Burger." Space-time then implodes into darkness.

Another indeterminate interval of time passes, and Jesse finds herself in front of the module's window, facing what appears to be a rotating anomaly outside that reflects a flash, traveling within the wave of a voice, both of which lodge into her mind:

"In the eighth invisible sphere lies the threshold. Worlds communicate through their mirrors. Knowledge is a bridge between life and death."

Jesse Kuunainen understands and places the octagon on the glass of her helmet. In the midst of the blackness, she perceives something or someone approaching, moving towards her own reflection. The polygonal object begins to spin with centrifugal force of its own.

Space and Time

"Lux waits at the threshold of the spiral."

"Tnemadnuf"

Iósif Beliónov finds himself suspended above the ground, atop the same symbol through which he entered the ship: a circle inserted inside a triangle. Strips of what appears to be spongy black leather cling along his naked body and seem to emit whispers that speak to his skin. One of them pierces the base of his neck, and it's as if his vision is altered. With a jolt, the albino now perceives that he is in the center of an octagonal structure, formed by a labyrinth of concentric streets with mirrors as walls.

Seven beams of light of different colors are projected from each of the nearest mirrors, hitting Iósif's body. A vibration strikes the interior of his brain, and then the walls of the large octagon begin to rotate, the beams of light converging into a circle that, thanks to the kinetics of the contraption, get closer and closer to form a massive white globe containing the albino's body.

"The Moon is in Yesod."

The rabbi's words in Iósif's memory seem to be uttered now, at the moment when, in the distance of the neutral space that surrounds him, a huge humanoid figure appears, a statue made of what appears to be solid, polished metal, with a head and limbs but without distinct or defined features.

Something compels the Soviet soldier to walk toward this kind of metallic, robotic golem, and the consequence is that several projections of himself advance in space, forming a straight line, as if several mirrors with his image were moving in front of him. The symmetrical movements of his replicas seem to follow a pattern that his mind has not marked for them.

Someone decides that they should stop, and then a face made up of points of light materializes on the head of the lifeless statue, with a single eye shining like a star, and words in an unknown language are written in the air of the abyss that seems to be its mouth.

"Ni eht hthgie elbisivni erehps si eht dlohserht. Sdlrow etacinummoc hguorht rieht srorrim. Egdelwonk si a egdirb neewteb efil dna htaed."

Iósif's flesh decomposes into similar letters that spread through the neutral space and begin to combine to form the interior and hull of a particle ship, filling in the gaps between them with numbers. The shining face of the statue is now part of the luminous body of a giant humanoid.

"Xul stiaw ta eht dlohserht fo eht larips."

Two galaxies in the shape of indescribable serpents or dragons battle, entwining themselves in the spiral of paradoxical connections.

Between the material and astral ship, a toroidal collision event occurs. In the molecular center of impact, in the space left between the two cones of spacetime repelling each other to infinity, an alternative fold opens up like a polar center in which Jesse and Iósif's matters intertwine and interpenetrate in symmetrical translation.

Their particles shape the curves of the torus with a cadence of disintegration-integration, their bodies intertwining in fractal strings that give them form, completing the physical cycle of a union of matter and antimatter within whose vibrational field positrons dance until mutual understanding is achieved.

"The vertebral column of the zodiac, carrying the souls of humans in the form of messages. That's what you call the "frontier," but for the Inner Empire, there are no boundaries."

Jose Ángel Conde Blanco has developed an extensive literary underground career in narrative, poetry and journalism, collected in many anthologies such as Gritos sucios, Beyond the Flesh, CyberTerror, Crimini amorosi and magazines Tentacle Pulp, El Tunche, Círculo de Lovecraft, Materia Oscura, The Wax, Serial Killer Magazine. Moreover he has published the novels Pleamar and Hela and four digital poetry books.

Diffusion
Brian U. Garrison

I've been thinking about the flavor of sunshine.
I've been wondering whether tulips dream
while they hibernate beneath the winter storms.

I've been hoping the frog song could carry me away
to roast marshmallows over distant stars. I've been
meaning to patch up my brain and hold my thoughts together,

but they keep leaking out into the world turning stop signs
into red lizards that scurry under speeding cars
and screech with the ferocity of tires on cement.

When my thoughts escape, the cars turn into flowers
and softly erupt in a splash of violets and greens
in a scene that would make any Elizabethan gardener jealous.

There's no containing unreality; no disillusionment spell
that I'm aware of, but the magpies build their nests
just as squarely with or without my constant observation.

I heard the little girl got caught in the big
M. C. Childs

The young lady who fell from a star
Wearing a light blue gingham dress

She was hungry
In the middle of a tornado

She has a basket
A couple of brand-new straws

Consulting with the rain
She's somewhere out in the storm

What makes the dawn come up like thunder?
All you do is follow the yellow brick road

Have the effrontery to ask for a brain
Dare to ask me for a heart

(Recomposed line fragments from The Wizard of Oz (Film),
Victor Fleming Director, 1939)

Space and Time

TAKE TWO ON THE MOVIES
Notes on "The Invisible Man"

When it comes to fantastic cinema, any discussion focusing on pre-war Hollywood usually centers on Universal's series of horror films especially "Dracula" and "Frankenstein" (both 1931), "The Mummy" (1932), "The Bride of Frankenstein" (1935), and "The Wolfman" (1941). With the exception of the Frankenstein movies, these were straight out horror films about vampires and curses and being bitten by a werewolf. The Frankenstein movies are arguably science fiction — author Brian Aldiss declared Mary Shelley's novel the birth of modern science fiction — but not to the general public. For most people, including many film critics, these were "monster movies." Indeed, in our modern video age these films were packaged as "Universal Classic Monsters."

The one film that cannot be treated as anything except science fiction is the 1933 adaptation of H. G. Wells' "The Invisible Man." Like "Frankenstein" and "Bride of Frankenstein" it features a scientist who is arguably mad and lusting after forbidden knowledge, but unlike in those films the "monster" here is none other than the scientist himself. Although the story and concept has been done many times since then, both on film and for television, the classic movie remains fresh and compelling today, nearly a century later. It remains highly regarded and it's worth exploring why.

The story opens at night in an English village pub that's filled with the expected stereotypical characters. Suddenly the door opens, and a mysterious figure appears, his head swaddled in bandages and his eyes hidden by dark glasses. He demands a room and food and, most importantly, to be left alone. What we soon discover is that, underneath these coverings, he is invisible. Jack Griffin (Claude Rains) has discovered a formula that will render people invisible. Now he is trying to come up with the antidote. What he does not realize is that one of the chemicals he is using is driving him insane.

Rains was a stage actor who had appeared in an obscure silent movie more than a decade earlier but was now launching a distinguished Hollywood career that would come to include movies like "Mr. Smith Goes to Washington," "Casablanca" and "Lawrence of Arabia." He not only had the title role here but got star billing, sharing the title card with author H. G. Wells. Ironically, audiences would not get to see the actor's face until the final moments of the film, after Griffin has died and the invisibility has worn off.

Notable is the setting of the story. Hollywood's horror and science fiction films of the era were almost always set outside of the United States. Movies like "The Mummy" and "King Kong" take place in Africa (although Kong would be transported to New York for his fatal rendezvous at the Empire State Building). More often these stories of the weird and horrific were stories about the Old World: "Dracula," "Frankenstein," "Freaks," "Phantom of the Opera," "The Hunchback of Notre Dame, "Dr. Jekyll and Mr. Hyde," "The Black Cat," "The Devil Doll," "The Invisible Ray" and many others. Contrast that with the films of a couple of decades later where, more often than not, the action took place in the United States. Even a movie like "The Thing," set at the North Pole, takes place at an American outpost. One possible reason for the difference is how Americans viewed the world at the time. In the 1930s, America looked at the rest of the world from a distance. A story set overseas was automatically exotic or alien whether it was Transylvania or, as here, an English village. American science was about inventors like Thomas Edison and Alexander Graham Bell. Placing the mad scientists in Europe made them that much stranger. One of the rare examples of a domestic mad scientist, "Dr. X" (1932), might be set in New York but the title character was played by the English actor Lionel Atwill preserving that sense of otherness.

As is befitting the pre-war "mad scientist" movies, the theme of forbidden knowledge is a major thrust of the film. "He meddled in things man was meant to leave alone," says one character of Griffin's research. Griffin had been working for Dr. Cranley (Henry Travers), whose kindly demeanor suggests someone who knows and respects those limits. He helps establish the alien science theme by noting that Griffin had been experimenting with "monocaine," a chemical that is derived from a plant in India. As if that wasn't foreign enough, Cranley has discovered the details about the negative properties of the drug from an obscure research article that had only been published in German. Clearly it is a substance that a respectable English-speaking scientist should avoid.

(If Dr. Cranley seems familiar it's because actor Henry Travers would go on to his most memorable role as the angel Clarence in "It's a Wonderful Life." Besides such Universal horror stalwarts as Una O'Connor and E.E. Clive, the film also has uncredited early performances by Walter Brennan as a man whose bicycle is taken by Griffin and John Carradine as someone suggesting using ink to reveal their invisible quarry.)

Audiences at the time thrilled to the creative and still impressive special effects which not only included objects seeming to move by themselves when handled by the invisible Griffin, but scenes

where he removes some of his bandages and/or his clothes while the rest of his outerwear remains visible. The film's release two years before the industry's censorious Production Code went into effect presumably allowed them to get away with the clear implication that when Griffin is completely unseen it's because he's stark naked.

What stands out today is that the script thoroughly examines what it would mean if such an invisibility potion was real. Griffin forces Dr. Kemp (William Harrigan)—Cranley's other assistant—to help him with his increasingly mad plans. He explains that he must remain covered after eating, since the food in his stomach would be visible until it is digested and absorbed. He notes that his presence can be given away by rain, fog, or smoke. Proving the point, he is later betrayed when his footsteps can be seen in the snow. Griffin (and the screenwriters) have clearly thought this through as he notes, "Even the dirt under my fingernails would give me away." Apparently being totally invisible requires more than just an injection. While Griffin is looking for an antidote—"There's got to be a way back," he declares—it is so he will gain total control of the process. As he goes mad, he declares his intention to use his power to rule, "To have the world grovel at my feet." He proposes a reign of terror, of murders and destruction that ordinary people will be powerless to prevent. This plays out with the townspeople becoming increasingly fearful as they have no way of knowing if he's even present when they're making their plans against him. They are right to be fearful as all their clever plotting is unable to prevent him from carrying out his threat to kill Kemp.

The one person who believes Griffin can be rescued from his fate is Cranley's daughter Flora (Gloria Stuart) who is with him when he's on his deathbed at the hospital dying from his gunshot wounds. In an ironic twist his invisibility now seals his fate since the doctors are unable to operate on his invisible lungs. It is only in death that the process reverses and he, at last, becomes visible again.

"The Invisible Man" is of a piece with many of the other films of era in positing that some knowledge is strange and forbidden, and those who fail to heed the warnings against invisibility serums, reanimating corpses, or capturing giant apes, will be lucky to survive the inevitable bad end in store for mere mortals who presume to know otherwise. By the 1950s the world was a different place with atomic energy and the Cold War paving the way for the monsters and aliens who now showed up on American doorsteps. The New World would no longer be safe from such threats.

Daniel M. Kimmel is the 2018 recipient of the Skylark Award, given by the New England Science Fiction Association. He was a finalist for a Hugo Award for *Jar Jar Binks Must Die… and other Observations about Science Fiction Movies* and for the Compton Crook Award for best first novel for *Shh! It's a Secret: a novel about Aliens, Hollywood, and the Bartender's Guide*. He is the author of several novels and short stories. His latest book is a film criticism parody, *Can Your Heart Stand the Shocking Facts?* about "Plan 9 from Outer Space."

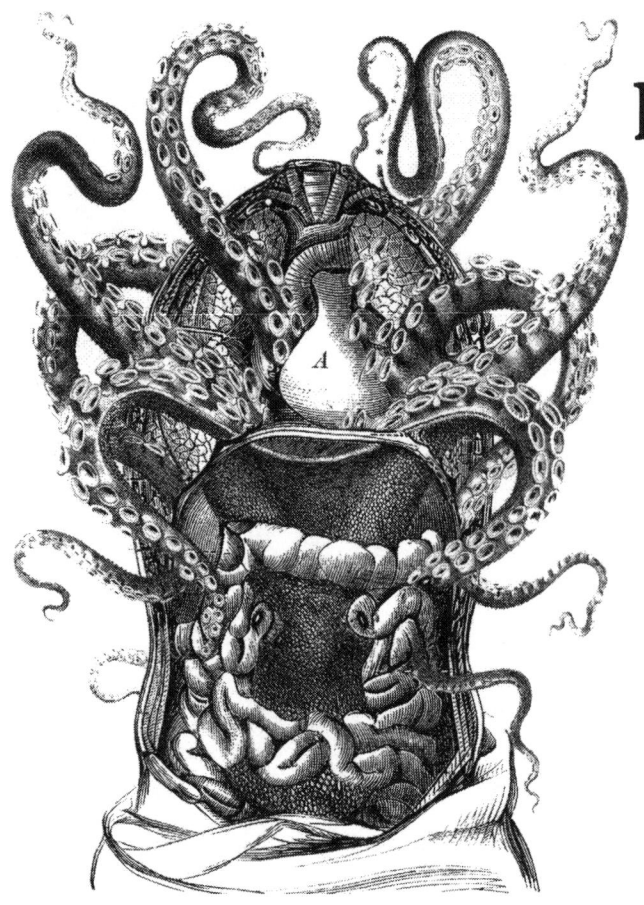

Death awaits like a shipwreck gently sinking into the cosmic abyss

Here at Space and Time we seek literary outliers. We welcome poetry, art and fiction that bend rules, transcend genre and break stereotypes.

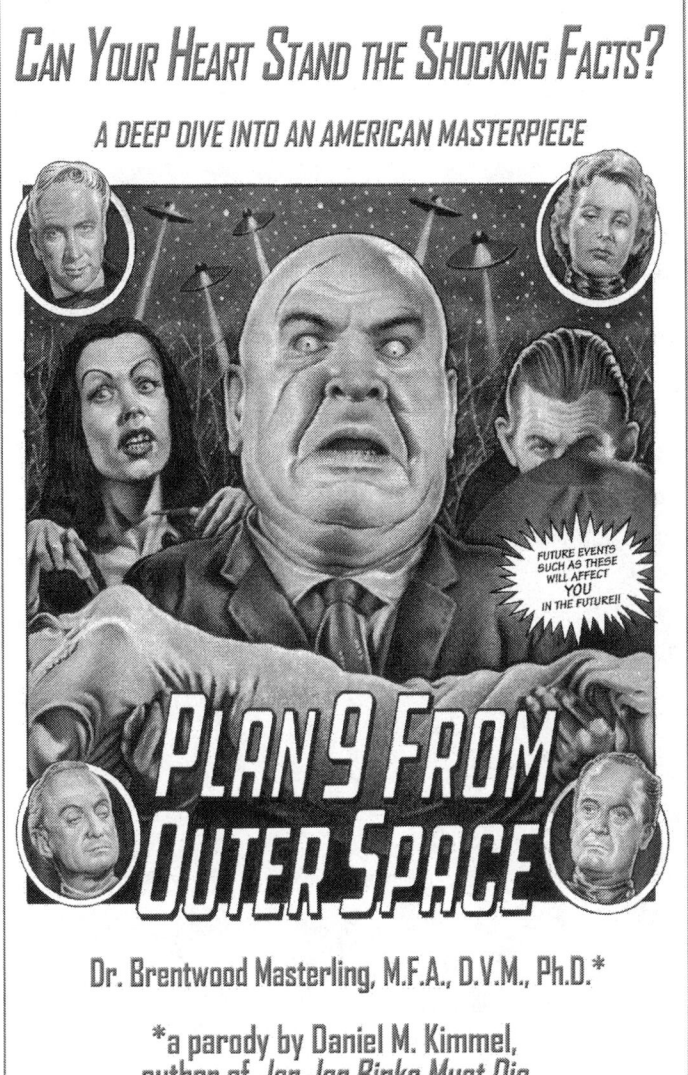

Can Your Heart Stand the Shocking Facts?
A DEEP DIVE INTO AN AMERICAN MASTERPIECE

Plan 9 From Outer Space

Dr. Brentwood Masterling, M.F.A., D.V.M., Ph.D.*

*a parody by Daniel M. Kimmel, author of Jar Jar Binks Must Die

Daniel M. Kimmel has made us think about movies as the veteran critic who wrote the Hugo finalist *Jar Jar Binks Must Die... and other observations about science fiction movies*. He's made us laugh as the author of *Shh! It's a Secret: a novel about aliens, Hollywood, and the Bartender's Guide*, *Time on My Hands: My Misadventures in Time Travel*, and *Father of the Bride of Frankenstein*. Now, for the first time anywhere, in the guise of his pompous alter ego Dr. Brentwood Masterling, M.F.A., D.V.M., Ph. D., he gets to do both.

Can Your Heart Stand the Shocking Facts? is indeed a "deep dive" into the world of director Edward D. Wood, Jr.'s Golden Turkey Award winner for Worst Film, *Plan 9 from Outer Space*. In it, Dr. Masterling provides an annotated complete transcript of the movie, along with an essay about Wood, and several questions for further discussion. Herein you'll learn how star Bela Lugosi cleverly died before the film was even made, and how Plan 1 had been to bring a gift basket to Earth. Is any of it true? As the Amazing Criswell asks in the film's stirring climax, "Can you prove that it didn't happen?"

"A fun, meta-satirical, faux-scholarly, bizarro-world critique of Ed Wood's classic flick."
—Hugo- and Nebula-Award winner David Brin

"A combination of classic parody with the panache of satire and the sparkle of a good zinger every now and again, this faux PhD thesis on the worst movie ever made strikes knowingly home."
—critic and author Nat Segaloff

"Kimmel's analysis is laugh-out-loud funny!"
—Michael A. Ventrella, author of *Big Stick*

"*Can Your Heart Stand the Shocking Facts?* is not for the faint-hearted—because they might collapse with hysterical laughter while reading it. Whether you love, hate, or love-hate Ed Wood's legendary disaster, be prepared for a whole new take, thanks to extensive annotations. Kimmel wields a razor-sharp pen on a very, very blunt object."
—Randee Dawn, author of *Tune in Tomorrow*

pdf available exclusively from www.FantasticBooks.biz

FANTASTIC BOOKS

Can Your Heart Stand the Shocking Facts?
by Daniel M. Kimmel
published by Fantastic Books
112 pages, trade paperback, $12.99
ISBN: 978-1-5154-5803-6

THIS UNIVERSE IS YOURS TO EXPLORE.

"There is a whole mythos to be uncovered in these pages... Is it good? Yes. But not easy. Not comfortable. It is creepy as hell. It is uncomfortable. Sink or swim, reader. You'll be glad you took the plunge."
—Jonathan Chapman
The Horror Zine

15 never-before-seen tales of cosmic horror from

Jonathan Maberry,
Laird Barron, Hailey Piper,
Brian Evenson,
Kristi DeMeester

and many more masters of the macabre.

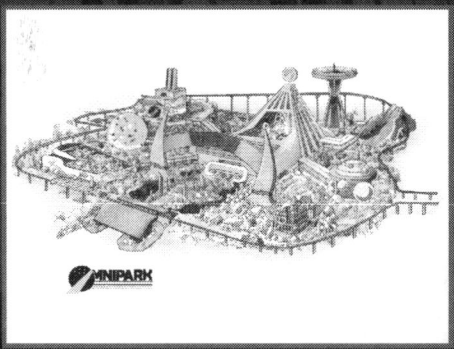

BACK 2 OMNIPARK

From 1977 to 2003, OmniPark thrilled, astonished, and educated guests of all ages ...or did it?

Are you brave enough to enter the world's weirdest theme park? Each story in this anthology reveals more of OmniPark's secret and terrifying history. What is the significance of the park's seven realms? What went on in the top-secret VIP area known as The Realm Between the Realms? How did globe-trotting oil billionaire Dalton Teague meet his wife and co-founder Evelyn — and what did they get up to on their clandestine travels to hostile deserts and jungles? What is the true and ultimate purpose behind OmniPark?

JUST, LIKE, DON'T

Written by Dom Gerard

Illustration by Prettysleepy Art via pixabay.com

So, I didn't even realize it when Brittney turned me into an alien. TikTok was like, #EndOfTheWorld #AlienInvasion, and I'm like, okayyy but I needed to post my next restaurant review. But then Brittney was like, I need to come over, I'm scared, and I'm like, of what, and she's like, aliens duh. So, I told her fine, even though it's late, mom isn't even home, and this guy on Grindr wants it and I'm so ready, but then she's like, for real, I'm legitimately triggered by everything that's going on, and I'm like, ughhh okay. So, we're hanging out, but cute Grindr boy is totally dtf, but fucking Brittney is like, just one more episode of RPDR, and I'm like, who even watches the Canadian version? And then she's like, wow, I do not feel good, and I'm like, okay, and she says, do my eyes look weird to you? At first, it's like, no Brittney, they're your eyes, they look the same. But then I really look, and there's like eyes behind her eyes, like millions of eyes, like she contained multitudes. Then I woke up, and she's all, isn't that better? And I was like, did you slip me molly? And Brittney laughed, but her voice had so many different notes to it, and she said that I was a part of the one now, which is like, okay sure, but does it get me into Nobu? She kept saying it's all going to be better now, and I'm, like, don't try to justify fucking mouth raping me or whatever the fuck you just did, and she's like, no seriously, it's going to feel amazing. Then she's like, let's go do someone.

Hot Grindr boy was still up, so we went over to his place, and he was like, why is your girlfriend here, and I said she likes to watch, and he was like, okay weird. We got naked, and he was like, you're so fucking gorgeous, and I was like, thank you hot yoga, and all I wanted to do was suck him off until I didn't, which was wild because I love sucking guys, but my body within my body wanted me to impregnate his mouth, and I did and he passed out. I felt kinda bad because consent, you know? But Brittney was like, we gotta bounce, he'll be fine. So, we did. And then we're jumping from rooftop to rooftop, which was absolute fire. Brittney was laughing and I was too because we were like 19-year-old gay ass superheroes. Well, I was gay, and she was like, a queer ally or whatever.

We landed on this one roof, and our senses were on high alert, like, out of nowhere. We tried to figure out what was happening, why we were so attuned to the cosmos or whatever. Then, we felt these vibrations under us, so we peeled back the top of the roof because we're mad strong now. And like, no shit, my mom was under the roof. She'd been, like, turned into a vessel or something. Like, she was all encased in a shell and her body was just a huge fucking womb, and I could sense thousands of bugs inside of her, growing and shit. And she's moaning and crying and just kind of a hot mess. And she's like, baby noooo, and I'm like, baby no what? And she was seriously so upset, but I'm like, mom, you're literally a bug factory, why are you crying about me? Even though she couldn't move or control anything about herself, she knew what was happening and still had her soul or whatever? She kept going on and on about losing me, and for a second, I wanted to cry too. Like, seriously sob. But then I'm like, wait, I get to keep this tight body and thick ass, and now I can jump over buildings too? I'm good. But she wouldn't stop crying and the clock was ticking, so I told her bye and sorry I couldn't help, though I think I could have, but getting her out would kill her and all the alien bug babies and that was against the plan that I didn't really know but did sorta know, you know? So, Brittney rolled the roof back on top of mom, and we peaced.

We get to town, and there's a shelter set up in the high school gym. Real talk, I always hated that fucking gym and all those cunts who made my life hell. But now, it's like, I'm back bitches, did you miss me? Alien revenge porn for the win. But Brittney and I have to calm down and put on our scared faces. Checkpoints are set up with soldiers or whatever, and a couple of them are so fucking hot, and I'm like, I'm totally going to make you pregnant later. Brittney is like, stop fucking smiling, so I cry and it's better because everyone tries to help us. The soldiers are checking our arms, because they think spiny hairs on people's arms are the first sign, but those come later, and they really should be looking in our eyes, but they don't know that yet. They'll figure it out at some point, but by then it'll be too late. I'm so itchy to get started, and Brittney is like, just, like, don't, we need to fucking wait. So, we keep crying, and I say something about missing my mom, though I don't really feel it anymore. Like, despite everything, she's really contributing, you know? We're both making a difference.

It's so hot in the gym, which is just perfect. We waited so long to come to Earth, because it needed to get hotter, and we knew the humans would keep on fucking shit up until it was ideal. If they knew better, they'd run to Canada, but they won't, and it's getting hot there too. Like, this is all going so well, right?

Dom Gerard lives in Philadelphia with his husband. Dom is the father of two incredible young people. His autobiographical essay "How Far 'Out' Do You Have To Be?" was published in the anthology *One Teacher in Ten in the New Millennium* in 2015. After a career in education, he works as a fiction writer.

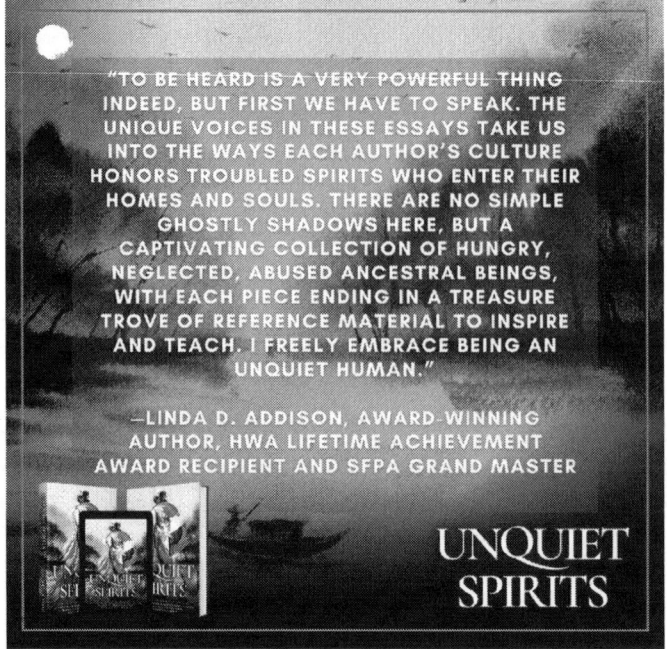

Grandi Successi

Written by Edoardo Maroncelli

Illustration by Prettysleepy Art via pixabay.com

When word got out that the famous Italian-American writer Joe Persico had bought the villa next door to ours, all the middle-aged women in the village went crazy with joy; a visit from the Pope would have caused less of a stir. And to think we were so proud of Bishop Rosetti, our fellow townsman, who had become a big shot in the Vatican in the 1970s.

San Tanero, a dot on the map of the Marche region, with four thousand inhabitants including dogs and cats, counted among its main attractions two cinemas, including the Lux which was about to be demolished, the Parish of Sant'Antonio, and the brand-new shopping center, Il Faggio, which looked like an alien cathedral, beautiful to behold but still empty after three years, with all those rows of shops with white signs and endless corridors where we played football. In short, our town had never been in the spotlight, not even for a crime story or a third division volleyball team, but soon everything would change. Joe Persico!

Many were skeptical, they couldn't believe it: It will end up like the shopping center... people would say on the Corso, where people paraded on Sundays in their best clothes, all show and no substance. But it was all true, the star of romance fiction, who came from Florida, so said the newspaper, arrived in San Tanero early one morning, in the middle of summer, in an unremarkable Opel, without drawing attention; perhaps he had chosen that house for his summer vacation, even though the sea was about twenty kilometers from the center. He could have gone to the Caribbean, but no: a small town in Italy, where not even the Middle Ages had passed, and there was really nothing to see.

He must have really wanted to be alone, away from popularity and the glitzy, noisy metropolises, perhaps to write a new novel. The fact is, my mother, a tailor with golden hands, shy and neglected, who never had anything new to show off in church, had suddenly become the most sought-after woman in town. Living on Via delle Magnolie next to Joe Persico, and especially owning that small kitchen from which one could see the writer's study, there on the second floor of the villa, had changed the game. My mother even became more beautiful, cultured, and perhaps even taller. The magic of Persico!

All the women from forty to seventy years old competed to become her friend, and thus be admitted to that female masonry that my father and I called the Kitchen of Espionage. They were organized with a couple of binoculars and savory pies, sweets, cookies, lasagnas, herbal teas, and every kind of godsend that each brought early in the morning, right after dawn, on large trays covered with aluminum foil.

Space and Time

They looked like priestesses, virgins with menopause, who prepared offerings for a pagan god. The husbands were not at all happy, forced to go eat in a trattoria, but it would have been risky to grumble too much, and risk ending up in the hands of those extremists: they would not hesitate to use their own men as human sacrifices, if it could somehow extend Joe Persico's stay in the village.

In addition to Mrs. Tassinari, a childhood friend of my mother, with thick hair above her upper lip that made her look like a carabiniere, in charge of booking the only bathroom in the house, and my aunt Santa, fat and always optimistic, the group included the rich women of the village, the Grilli sisters, Marta and Addolorata, owners of the Supermarket Arlecchino, the envious Mrs. Piccioni and Stradalti with their theatrical hairstyles, and other women I had never seen before.

Dad ended up like the others, no longer the center of attention when he came home from the factory, and as he dared to step into the kitchen for a well-deserved beer he felt like a pin cushion, with all those eyes on him that seemed to say: Don't you have anything else to do?

"Those women have lost a Thursday, my son," he would decree every evening seated in front of the television, comfortable on the green velvet armchair with a remote-controlled backrest. He just couldn't understand those women, he was practically immune to literature, so much so that I had never seen him open a book, not even by mistake.

He much preferred to cling to the television, what my mother called the Brain-Annihilator, and his beloved boxing matches, cycling races, noisy western movies, and infomercials for technological gadgets. His world was those images, so colorful, lively, and vibrant, far from pages full of words and lies, tiring to read with the spirit numbed by ten hours in front of a lathe.

My room was right above the kitchen, and for weeks I enjoyed listening to the women's fantasies about their favorite writer. When you're eleven years old, and you live in a small town like me, there's not much better to pass the time. The bike, video games, and the chatter of my mother's friends: these had become the staples of my free time.

"You can't help but love a man who understands women so well," I heard Mrs. Tassinari say, who eventually shaved her mustache, and my mother immediately added, making me jump: "You're right, I'd go with him to the ends of the earth, forget about washing underwear!" And then laughter.

Talks became increasingly surreal and sentimental, just like Joe Persico's books.

"If I found myself in front of him, I wouldn't be able to open my mouth, like a teenager on a first date," once revealed Marta Grilli, who had her underwear washed by a part-time girl. And then hours and hours talking about those syrupy novels, from *You're Special* to *Last Night of Passion*, of which I had seen a copy on the sofa in the living room, at least seven hundred pages, with a cover featuring a languid kiss, painted in watercolors, between lovers not so young anymore, emulating the pose of the sailor and the nurse from the famous photo in Times Square. But the war had been over for a long time.

"Those women have lost a Thursday, my son," my father said again one evening. He couldn't take it anymore. "Want to take a walk?" he added, turning off the Brain-Annihilator, which meant something serious was happening. He took me to the Bar 'Da Secondo', where all the neglected husbands of the village had taken refuge, the steel tables full of ashtrays, bottles of grappa, and playing cards, on the maxi screen the Inter match, and then we went in front of the shopping center and stood watching it for a long time, so empty and white like the funeral monument of an emperor, with a ceiling of stars.

"That damned liar, selling people fake life," he commented bitterly, showing me his hands marked by work, before returning home. Arriving in the driveway, we were surprised by the light off in the kitchen. We quickened our pace and entered on tiptoe, fearing the worst, only to discover that the house was empty, and all those women suddenly disappeared, including my mother.

"Dad, what do we do?" I said hesitantly, pointing to Persico's study, lights on as always, and he replied strangely "I don't want to know, go to sleep, you'll see that tomorrow all the fanfare of these fanatics will return, they can't do without it," before sitting in front of the Brain-Annihilator and turning on a replay of *Once Upon a Time in the West*, without saying another word.

He had disconnected his soul from his body, more than usual, and I understood; his little habits were essential not to poison his life too much, and he had lost them. But I had to do something. I ran out into the garden towards Persico's villa. A beautiful beech tree in front seemed to suit my purpose, to be able to see inside the illuminated study.

I climbed up and managed to find the right position, with my feet on two strong branches, and the incredible scene entered my eyes. Persico, standing in front of his desk, with the oval of his face featureless, black and dotted with stars and constellations, like the sky above the shopping center, and legs and arms made of twisted electrical cables.

In front of him a line of women, naked as priestesses, hair loose, waiting for their turn for something, which didn't seem good at all. It was my mother's turn at that moment, who passionately kissed that black hole of a face, immersing half of her face in it, before vanishing like a short circuit, sending many sheets flying around the room, a manuscript full of words, of her. It wasn't true what my father had said, Persico's novels didn't tell lies, they were real people, disillusioned with life, turned into words, pages, chapters.

All great successes.

Edoardo Maroncelli (Ravenna, Italy) is a dark fantasy and horror fiction writer. He attended the professional course at the Alessandro Manzetti Creative Writing Academy. His stories has been published in Italian on some magazine and anthologies. This is his first publication in English.

No matter what stage you are at in your writing career, the Horror Writers Association has a level for everyone. Consider joining today.

Want to get noticed?
Try advertising in Space & Time!

$150 for Full Page: 8.5 x 11
$75 for Half Page: 8.5 x 5.5
$45 for Quarter Page: 4.25 x 5.5

Black and white, camera ready ads only.

Visit
spaceandtime.net/advertise
to secure your ad now!

Creative Writing Academy
Courses for Professionals
Free Courses for Young Authors (Under 26)
in English and Italian
More Info: www.alessandromanzettiacademy.com

Plague Hag
KT Wagner

The plague hag returned. City condos for sale marked an exodus to suburbs, towns, and villages. A negligible commute when there's a network signal. Details worked out later.

Through history, mansion-like clergy homes crouched alongside church spires. A bell tower in every town, every village. The church wielded inordinate power.

City condo values declined. Country home values increased. Realtors nodded. Frowned. Latecomers to the migration, lowered expectations, open to possibilities.

The church preached conformity, adherence to roles and rules. Subservience to a God defined by men. Empires and institutions rose and fell.

A former church house, unoccupied more than a century. Requires renovation. Repairs. The intoxication of vast square footage. A silent garden. Blessed isolation.

Muttered rumour, ancient legends, curses. Warded by the sign of the cross. Houses shuttered against things which roam at night. Consecrated ground. Salted earth.

Tall tales the realtor claimed. Wild grains and grasses are healthy. Golden and eldritch purple seed heads ripe for harvest. Elbow grease. Sweat equity. A steal.

Everything of value in the parish houses auctioned off, buildings gutted. Sheets shrouded the remains. Rodents and spiders multiplied. Thrived.

A hearth fire crackled, incinerating the former occupants of the chimney. Cleaning and demolition first. Clear an area to sleep, an area to eat.

Local tradesmen refused work at the church house, warned off by fathers, uncles and brothers. Best leave it be. They muttered. Spat on the ground.

A wooden box sealed and buried. Mourning rings studded with teeth. Finger bones. A glass eye. Stained room behind a basement brick wall. Rusty tools, tatters of rotted fabric.

Enlightenment flowed and ebbed. Church membership plummeted. Rural populations fled for the city. The church divested. Hiding the sins buried beneath.

A glass eye dangled from a silver chain, its iris a storm-grey abyss. City friends tittered over flutes of chardonnay, homemade biscuits. Their dancing frenzied.

Photo by Lars (aka LN_Photoart) via pixabay.com

Reticent locals, wary of outsiders, maintain their distance. No talking. No shouting. Absolutely no singing. Or dancing. Move on quickly.

A screech of agony. An owl, not a human. A yowl. A cat, not a demon. Rabbits not unheard of. But there'd never been tell of one that big.

Warnings issued. Pagan healers, the full moon, seductresses, heretics, and sorcery. Keep women and girls inside. Under control. Education, power, opinions, all handled by men.

Whispers curled through keyholes. Mournful words tumbled, landed with a splat. Sour milk soaked into pounded chalk. Names. Birthdates. Occupations. Deaths.

Sidonia. Noblewoman, femme fatale. Beheaded and burned.
Agnes. Healer. Strangled and burned.

An ivy tunnel connected to a secret garden. Encircled in stone. Fed by a burbling spring. Sulphur, monkshood, belladonna, and water hemlock. Alluring. Deadly.

Anna. Servant. Decapitated.
Michée. Washerwoman. Hanged and burned.

Names spooled, curled, through cracks and vents. Landed in tangled clumps. A hardware store in the city sold a grey putty. Guaranteed to fix leaks and holes.

Bridget. Tavern owner. Hanged.
Sarah. Housewife. Mother. Hanged.

Shadows revealed a corner shelf no one could reach. Where there is no light, the silhouette of a poppet. Pinched. Choked. Bitten.

Outsiders never stayed long. The villagers knew this but never spoke of it, lest it draw unwanted attention.

Times passed. The plague hag gathered broom and rake, then retreated. Villagers mingled, cautious. Stories were spun of city dwellers who came and went.

Again, a realtor pounds a battered for-sale sign into the weedy lawn of the church house.

INUJINI JUNE 23, 2024

Three indigenous Shimanchu girls are stripped of everything in a war their people will gain nothing from except loss. As they struggle to survive, they learn the power of resilience lies in connecting with who they were, who they are and who they will be together.

YURIKOPUBLISHING.COM

The Ring of Destiny

Written by **Michael H. Payne**
Illustrated by Anthony R. Rhodes

The figure standing in the moonlight on the forest path ahead of her didn't much startle Sarah.

Yes, it was odd that the shadows from the flat-brimmed black hat still somehow let her see the black mask, cape, and boots the figure was also wearing. And yes, it was odd that it was a foot-and-a-half tall hedgehog standing on its hind legs: hedgehogs weren't native to southern California, after all.

But how could it possibly be anything threatening? This was the patch of forest at the end of Sarah's street, the patch she'd walked in every night after supper for nearly four decades. She'd grown up here, had gone to school across town, had inherited the house when first Mom and then Dad had died, had worked giving eye exams at Dr. Napoor's optometry office just down the road for twenty years. She couldn't imagine this place *not* being safe—except from drought and global warming and all the vast, nearly incomprehensible worldwide threats that drove Sarah to watch cartoons almost every night.

"So," a low voice said then, the hedgehog shifting ever so slightly. "That's you at last, is it?"

The Cockney accent tickled Sarah's ear. "I'm sorry?" she asked, looking around for anyone who might be hiding among the rows of trees. "Is this a weird joke or something?"

"Oh, it's weird," the voice went on, and the hedgehog began to walk toward her, its upright posture apparently not bothering it at all. "And it's definitely something. But a joke? That depends." It stopped in front of her, its head tipped back so Sarah could see its mouth moving in perfect synchronization with the words she was hearing. "You finding it funny at all?"

"In a way," she had to admit. Sarah was a firm believer in honesty whenever possible. "I mean, 'funny' doesn't always mean humorous, so it could be...one of the other...definitions..."

She swallowed. The hedgehog's eyes, as shiny as wet stones in the moon's silver glow, were making her realize once and for all that this was *not* some neighborhood kid in a costume. She was really standing here talking to a big hedgehog dressed as Zorro. And while she didn't think she'd get an honest answer, she decided to ask the question twitching in her head like a bird that had just bounced off a plate glass window. "Am I going crazy?"

Despite not having much in the way of shoulders, the hedgehog shrugged. "Not my department," he said—that deep voice, she decided, meant it was male. He doffed his hat and gave a bow. "I'm here to sweep you off on a magical adventure, y'see, so I'm likely not qualified to answer."

Sarah nodded. "And are we leaving right away?" She gestured to her blue jeans and burgundy sweater. "I'm not really dressed for any sort of magical adventure." She perked a bit. "Unless clothing will be provided?"

The hedgehog blinked, his little ears falling where they stuck up through slits around the crown of his hat. "Just like that?" he asked. "One little 'am I crazy,' and you're ready to take off with the first talking hedgehog you meet?"

She didn't *mean* to make a rude noise, blowing air through her lips, but she didn't feel the need to apologize when she did. "This sort of thing happens pretty regularly in cartoons and books," she told him before a thought struck her and made her blink. "Or are you saying this is your first time?"

His eyes widening, his mouth opened, but no words came out.

"And yes," Sarah went on, not sure why she kept explaining things to him: maybe because it seemed unlikely that he was familiar with Earth's popular culture, or maybe because he'd looked cuter before he'd come all over confused, "I know that comics and movies and such aren't *real*. I haven't been expecting ghosts or space aliens or hedgehogs to pop up and call me the chosen one or anything. But now that it *has* happened, well, I can't pretend I haven't thought about it. It'd be like having a genie appear when you rub an old bottle and then not having your three wishes all ready to go." She shook her head. "Because *everybody's* thought about *that*."

The hedgehog managed to look more confused than ever. "You mean you've planned out what you're gonna do if you ever summon a genie? Even though there aren't any actual genies anywhere near this plane of existence?"

Sarah folded her arms. "There aren't any talking hedgehogs around here, either."

Things got quiet then: externally, all Sarah could hear was the indistinct muttering of someone's TV through the trees off to her right. *Internally*, though, she was simply crowing, her fists wanting to pump and her tennis shoes wanting to stomp. Because, while the vast majority of her mind and spirit as far back as the second grade had accepted that magical adventures didn't actually happen, a minority opinion holding the exact opposite view had forever been floating around her brain like the tiniest possible firefly. And now?

Without an instant's hesitation, Sarah pulled that small glowing part of herself out of its corner and gave it her whole brain. After all, the quicker she figured out the details of this magical adventure, drawing on the knowledge she'd been accumulating since she first read *The Wizard of Oz* or imagined meeting Kimba the White Lion, the more likely she'd be able to beat whatever villain she'd inevitably run across.

"All right, then!" The hedgehog's sudden smile puffed into Sarah's face like a breath of pine-scented air, startling her out of her thoughts. "Haxon's the name," he said, standing on the tiptoes of his boots to stretch up his right front paw. "I think you're gonna be exactly what we need in Azuredale."

With a nod, Sarah bent at the knees and waist to reach her index and middle fingers down toward him. "I hope so," she said. "It'd be an awful waste of time if I weren't. Still—"

She'd been about to ask if he had some sort of magic portal he could open to take them through to the talking animal world where this adventure would happen, but the instant his claws closed around the tips of her fingers, everything went black. The ground slipped away under her tennis shoes, pushing her breath out in a gasp that didn't leave anything behind for words, wind swirling, a warm rush completely out of keeping with the cool November evening. His voice, however, sounded even clearer than before in her head:

That ring you've got on.

A sudden shimmer pulled her attention down to her left hand and her great-aunt's little diamond floret ring. She'd always imagined that she would give it to the man who presented her with an engagement ring, but, well, it had never spent any appreciable time over the past two decades anywhere other than her finger and its black-velvet-lined case on her nightstand.

When the time comes, Haxon's voice went on, *and you'll know it when it does, focus your belief in what's true and important through that ring, and you'll save us all.*

Not sure how to respond—or even where her mouth was, for that matter—she watched the diamond ring fade away before an orange glow faded in, rough stone columns where the trees had been standing half a moment before. The floor and ceiling seemed to be stone as well, and the glow, she could now see, was coming from torches the size of toothbrushes sticking out from some of the columns.

Sarah nodded to Haxon, the hedgehog still holding

her hand. "Telepathy and dimensional teleportation. Very nice. And you've definitely got the ambience down here." She sniffed the air, just sooty and dry enough to tickle her nose but not make her sneeze. "You said it was a magical adventure, after all, not some sort of horrible realistic scenario."

"Ummm...," Haxon began, but a higher-pitched voice cut him off:

"Horrible? Realistic?" Something green and gold flashed in the torchlight, and a hummingbird as large as two clenched fists whisked up in front of her. The bird was wearing a green cocked hat and a golden belt with a little crossbow and a quiver of bolts hanging from it. "The last eight months around have a been more horrible and more real than anything I've ever seen in my whole entire life! So don't try to—!"

"It's all right, Pidge." Haxon let go of Sarah's hand and stepped away, a tiny thumb unfolding from the side of his paw to point at her. "Sarah here's just what they call 'genre savvy.' She knows all about talking animal people coming to take her on magical adventures, doesn't she?"

"Hey!" Sarah felt a blush heating her ears. "Look, I'm sure your dark overlord or whatever it is that's driven you out of your charming little villages in the woods and forced you into these cold and dusty tunnels in the mountains—"

"What?" the hummingbird squeaked again, zooming to hover a couple inches from Sarah's face. "Are you a *spy?*" With another colorful flash, the bird was gripping the little crossbow in its feet, the string drawn back, a bolt in the groove, and the whole thing pointed directly at Sarah's right eye.

Different parts of her screamed contradictory advice as to whether ducking would help or would just trigger the bird into firing, so Sarah ended up standing stock still, her throat feeling like it had frozen solid. Haxon's voice, though, echoed around the cavern. "No, Pidge! Damn it, girl, she's not a—!"

"You sure, Hax?" And while Sarah had never had any reason to wonder if hummingbirds could growl, she now knew for certain that they could. "I pump a couple of these things into her skull, and we don't hafta to worry no more about—"

"Will you just—" Something was popping in and out at the bottom of Sarah's peripheral vision, and she forced herself to glance away from the suddenly-less-than-cute crossbow to see the hedgehog jumping up and down, flailing his hat in his front paws as if he were trying to swat the hummingbird with it. "I brung her here to *help!*"

Pidge's aim didn't waver. "Then why's she know about Darkfang? Why's she know about us hiding here in the caves while we plan the rebellion?"

"It happens a lot," Sarah heard herself say, and she would've clapped her hands over her mouth if she hadn't been afraid the movement might startle the hummingbird. Her mind was whirling, though, like her brain was strapped to a runaway carousel. "I've, uhh, studied the, uhh, the records about this sort of thing, and I...I want to help..."

For a long, long moment, only the hummingbird's wings moved, a buzzing blur behind her. Then she flashed again; Sarah winced, but the crossbow, instead of firing, now dangled empty and uncocked from Pidge's belt. "An apprentice hero?" The bird shrugged in a way that somehow didn't interrupt her hovering. "Better than nothing." A puff of dry air made Sarah blink, and then the space in front of her was empty. "Get her to the main chamber, Hax!" Pidge's voice came from somewhere to Sarah's right. "I'll call the council!"

It took one more long, long moment before Sarah managed to take her next breath. "That doesn't happen in the cartoons," she said once she could. "I mean, maybe I missed the cartoons where it does, but the crossbow? Right there? Pointed at my eye?" She raised a hand, slightly surprised that she could make it move, and waggled shaking fingers through the air where Pidge had been hovering. "That was really real," she finished, knowing how stupid it sounded but not able to find better words.

A sigh pulled her attention back to Haxon flopping his hat into place. "We're living a cliché," he said, looking up at her, "but we're *living* it, not watching it on the telly or reading about it in some book. So head in the game, all right?" He winked through his mask and turned to Sarah's right. "Now, remember your ring, and let's go meet the gang."

Most of the council meeting didn't much startle Sarah. After following Haxon through a series of low and winding torchlit tunnels, she stepped into another large cavern, and there, gathered around a rough stone table covered with even rougher maps, sat or stood or perched a dozen slightly-larger-than-normal woodland creatures: a fox vixen, several mice, a badger, a mole, some brownish-reddish-grayish birds who could've been anything from wrens to robins as far as Sarah knew, one bird who was definitely a crow or a raven, and one who was a hawk or a falcon, all of them wearing little hats or vests.

The cuteness almost got her squealing, but their unhappy expressions stopped her. The mix of predator and prey, too, as well as Haxon's Zorro outfit and the absolutely darling little kelly green Robin Hood tunic the vixen was wearing all gave more evidence that this was a *serious* magical adventure. They were obviously a rag-tag band of freedom fighters united against this villain Darkfang whom Pidge had mentioned.

Haxon introduced Sarah as someone "ready, willing, and able to help," and Sarah did her best not to let her doubts show. She nodded to them, and then sat listening as they took turns introducing themselves and speaking in solemn tones about Darkfang the Conqueror coming out of the east eight months ago and taking over most of Azuredale. The maps on the table turned out to be diagrams of Azuredale Castle, now Darkfang's citadel: the vixen, Princess Margo, explained how a still-unknown traitor had let Darkfang in and that, as far as she knew, she was the only one of the royal family to have escaped.

Pretty standard isekai/comic book/fairy tale stuff, all told. Still, every bit of information helped Sarah refine what type of adventure this actually was, and she had something of a hard time swallowing her grins as their story went on and she was able to add and discard possible future plot elements based on the shows and novels she'd seen or read.

But Sarah decided not to ask Princess Margo whether Darkfang had killed her parents or simply imprisoned them. Yes, that would go a long way toward telling her what level of violence she could expect here, but the princess's wavering eyes told her not to press the matter. She could ask Haxon later.

That there was a traitor involved, though, sharpened her gaze on the group in the chamber: more often than not, someone in the rebel high command was working with the villain. And sure enough, by the time the introductions had moved around the table—the last figure was someone large wearing a brown robe and cowl: a bear, Sarah figured—she'd become almost certain that the traitor was Durgis, the badger. He was paying really close attention to the plan for storming Darkfang's citadel even though he stayed out of the discussion, and a certain hardness came over him whenever he looked at Princess Margo.

It wasn't nearly enough for Sarah to leap up and denounce him in the middle of the meeting, of course. But it was something else to put on her list to discuss with Haxon.

That was when events startled her for the first time—other than the surprise of being pulled into a magical adventure in the first place. For when the figure in the brown robe stood and pushed back his cowl, he was as human as her.

"Godfrey Thorne," he said with a bow, his British accent more 'Masterpiece Theater' than Haxon's and his eyes a very deep bluish sort of green. He seemed to be about Sarah's age, too, a few wrinkles around his smile, his hair salt-and-peppery and just covering the tops of his ears.

She didn't want to stare, of course, but, well, in these sorts of magical adventures where someone from Earth came to a land of talking animals or elves or space aliens, the hero or heroine was always the only human. All the other characters were creatures indigenous to the magical world: that was just the way the stories *worked*. And yes, she hadn't watched or read them *all*, but if this place had humans, would she need to reevaluate her conclusions about what was happening here?

Still, she shook herself, made a few suggestions based on plans like this that she'd seen before—take advantage of the pipes that carried water into the castle, for instance, or carried sewage out—and got a lot of heads nodding in agreement with her points. But she found herself meeting Godfrey's pleasant eyes just about every time she looked around, something that almost set her to stammering more than once.

Even worse, when the meeting ended several hours later with the council voting unanimously to accept the newly modified attack plan, Sarah lost track of Haxon among the council members coming up to welcome her and thank her personally for her help. In fact, by the time the various winged and furred bodies had cleared out enough for her to take a good glance around, only Godfrey Thorne remained in the chamber with her.

The little half-smile that tugged his lips made her swallow; she'd given up on men, especially attractive ones, more than a decade ago. And sure, sometimes stories like this had one of the animal people getting a crush on the human, but that was just for comedy relief. What was she supposed to do now?

"Lady Sarah," he said with another little bow.

"No, no." She held up a hand. They had a princess, after all, so titles must mean something here. "I'm just a person who works with an—" She swallowed the word 'optometrist,' not sure if he'd understand it, and finished with, "an eye doctor."

His eyebrows went up. "My brother's an optician, actually, grinding lenses and all that." A frown pulled at his lips. "At least, I *suppose* he's still doing it. Darkfang's forces control our village, but, well, having slaves who can see what they're doing would be important, wouldn't it? When they're cutting down the trees or plowing the new fields, he wouldn't want their axes to go astray or their furrows to be crooked..." With a little laugh, he rubbed his forehead. "I think I'm officially rambling at this point. It's just..." His hand came down, revealing those lovely eyes. "I've nothing against animal folks, but I've not seen another human in eight months."

Sarah's chest tightened, her face going hot, and without thinking, she blurted out, "I think Durgis is the traitor!"

Godfrey blinked at her, and Sarah wanted to kick herself. It wasn't completely out of the question for the traitor in one of these stories to have an accomplice, after all, someone the heroine trusted only to have him turn on her in a last-minute plot twist. She hoped that Godfrey didn't fit that role, but since, strictly speaking, he shouldn't be here at *all*, she couldn't rule him out completely as a bad guy. So—

"Do you know where Haxon is?" she asked, pushing past him toward one of the tunnels that led out of the council chamber. "Or do you know any openings to the outside where Durgis could go to signal these new plans to Darkfang's forces?"

"Wait," he said behind her. "What?"

Fortunately, Sarah found Pidge and a large squirrel on guard in the corridor, and she shared her suspicions with the hummingbird. "Don't sound an alarm," she added quickly, "but can you—I don't know—send someone outside to check if anyone's sending messages to the castle?"

Pidge did another of her odd shrugs. "It's the middle of the night, so I shouldn't have any problem sneaking upstairs for a quick flight around to see if anything stinks." She winked at Sarah. "If Her Nibs or anybody complains, I'll say you told me to, and since you're the big hero, she'll hafta hold her tongue, won't she?"

Watching Pidge dart off down the rough-hewn hallway, Sarah couldn't keep from biting a fingernail. Behind her, she heard Godfrey say, "She'll be fine." A hand touched her elbow. "Perhaps you'd care to come back to my room and wait?"

Space and Time

All sorts of nerves twitched her away from him. "I'm sorry, Godfrey, but I'd rather be here when she comes back."

He nodded. "Then can I get you a cup of anything? A plate? You must've traveled quite a distance to—"

"Thank you but no." The clench in her throat went all the way down to her stomach. "I honestly don't think I'd be able to keep anything down right now."

Whether he nodded in response to this or not, Sarah didn't know: her feet forced her to turn and start pacing along the wall of the council chamber. Godfrey made a few more attempts to start a conversation, asking where she was from and how she'd heard of their plight, but that only startled her from her stewing thoughts—was she accusing an innocent badger of a terrible crime? All she could do was apologize some more, saying she couldn't really concentrate till Pidge returned.

Unless, of course, this was a more violent story than she thought. In which case, Pidge might not *be* returning...

She was just shaking her head to his offer of a chair when squawks and chitters flooded the hall. Sarah whirled toward the door, and a couple burly moles pushed Durgis into the chamber, the badger's front paws bound together with wire.

"He didn't have a chance!" Pidge buzzed in crowing like a soprano rooster. "I saw him flashing that lantern down the side of the mountain, so I grabbed it and smashed him over the head a couple times with it!"

The council came in behind the moles, Haxon beside Princess Margo. Fur and feathers ruffling, everyone took their places at the table except Godfrey, still standing along the wall beside Sarah, and Haxon started shouting questions at Durgis about who he'd been signaling and what he'd told them.

Durgis just stayed squatted on the stone floor between the moles, not answering or even raising his eyes. Haxon threatened him with declawing, whisker shaving, and imprisonment, but nothing happened; after a few minutes, his ears flat and his spines arched, Haxon fell huffing back into his seat as well.

That was when Princess Margo rose to her hind paws, her expression the same mix of wavering and hardness that Sarah had seen from her before. "Why, Durgis?" she asked quietly. "Why did you betray everyone and everything you've ever known?"

For the first time, Durgis looked up, his eyes dark and narrow. "Ask your mother, princess," he more growled than said. "She sealed the fate of Azuredale twenty years ago when she chose your father over me."

Fur bristled along the princess's neck. "Take him away," she whispered, and the moles hauled him out of the chamber.

Things stayed quiet for a long moment, part of Sarah whispering that this didn't make sense. Princess Margo's parents would both have to be foxes, so how could a badger—?

But Sarah quickly smothered every trace of that thought. Of *course* a romance gone wrong lay at the base of this whole terrible situation! For this kind of magical adventure story, it was absolutely perfect!

At that point, though, Princess Margo, her gaze still downcast, gave a sniffle and said, "So it's over. Darkfang knows everything, and we're...we're..." A sob swallowed whatever she'd been about to say.

"No!" Sarah hadn't meant to shout it, but pushing away from the wall, she found that she couldn't keep quiet, her great-aunt's ring tingling. "Durgis wouldn't have had time to send the changes to the plan that we made tonight, so Darkfang doesn't know anything more about it than he did before!"

More thoughts bubbled up, and she didn't even try to stop them from bursting out. "One thing he *has* to have known, though, is where you're holed up! I mean, he's been sending someone here for however many months to pick up Durgis's lantern signals, right? So if he's known where you are, why hasn't he attacked?" She looked around the whole assembly, their eyes wide and their ears partially down. "It's because he's *afraid* of you! Darkfang is *afraid!*"

A few ears twitched upward, a few whiskers stiffening. Refusing to let her voice or body shake no matter how wildly her heart was thumping, Sarah spread her hands. "We can take advantage of that fear if we attack right now. The plan I saw here earlier looks ready to go, so let's do it tonight!" She slapped a fist into the palm of her hand, and while it didn't make *that* much noise, several of the animals started back, the floret pattern of the diamonds on her ring shimmering across the cavern walls. "Darkfang'll be waiting for his spy to bring Durgis's news, and what he'll get instead is the entire rebel army sneaking in and breaking his stranglehold on Azuredale!"

Most of the animals were staring with open mouths, but Haxon and Godfrey both looked like they'd taken a punch to the stomach. From her post at the doorway, though, Pidge hollered, "Yes!" And when Sarah met Princess Margo's gaze, the fox vixen's eyes were practically blazing.

How the attack on the palace turned out didn't much startle Sarah, but she had to admit that the battle itself—what little she saw of it—was certainly dramatic.

She joined the princess, Haxon, Godfrey and several dozen woodland creatures wearing little pieces of chain mail and carrying little spears as they snuck through a weed-encrusted water gate on the riverbank and into the castle's fresh water pipes. She'd been able to hear Pidge's forces engaging with Darkfang's along the castle walls, and the plan called for the moles and their group to make their way up the sewer pipes at the same time to catch the invaders in a three-way pincher.

It went quite well, all things considered, but then Sarah hadn't really expected otherwise. Pidge took an arrow through one of her wings—there were always *some* injuries in these types of stories—but she managed to change her fall into a dive behind the battlements where she held off Darkfang's troops with swords clenched in her foot claws till Sarah's group and the band of moles broke in.

They surfaced in the castle courtyard very near to Pidge, and a single command of "Surrender!" from Princess Margo was enough to get the mice and squirrels and birds wearing Darkfang's black armor to throw down their weapons. Haxon used his magic to fix Pidge's wings while Sarah and Godfrey ran to the castle's gatehouse to let down the drawbridge.

That was when Darkfang himself attacked. He turned out to be a big, brown rabbit, and his sword fight with the princess really wrapped things up. Standing beside Godfrey on top of the gatehouse, Sarah watched breathless in spite of knowing the inevitable outcome. So when Princess Margo knocked Darkfang's sword out of his paw and the moles took him into custody, Sarah cheered right along with the rest of the rebels.

Princess Margo's reunion with her parents and her brother after the moles brought them up to the throne room from the dungeon was just as heartwarming. Sobbing and laughter mixed among the crowds of animal people, and with her throat tightening, Sarah started to reach for Godfrey's sleeve—

When she saw her ring glinting in the torchlight.

Hadn't Haxon said that she would need to use the power of the ring or something to defeat the villain? That was how it always worked in the stories and cartoons and comics, after all: the person on the magical adventure had been brought in to play an integral part in bringing peace and justice to the world!

Being taller than almost everyone, she easily found Haxon among the hugging royal foxes. But before she could take a step toward him through the furred and feathered folks, a loud sigh puffed out beside her, and the whole place froze, everyone suddenly silent and unmoving. "Damn it," a not-quite-familiar voice said. "You just had to ruin everything, didn't you?"

Spinning, Sarah found herself blinking at Godfrey, a pout on his face that she could only call petulant. "After all my trouble," he said, his British accent replaced by something plain and whiny and American, "why couldn't you be happy and do what you were supposed to, huh?"

And at that point, startled was much too small a word for what Sarah was feeling. "Godfrey?" she asked.

"Jim." He folded his arms. "Not that you care. You've been doing everything wrong ever since I brought you here!"

"*You* brought me? But—" Turning to look at Haxon, she blinked to see him step away from the motionless royal family, his ears down and his spines nearly flat.

"Who else?" Godfrey was saying—or Jim, Sarah supposed. He snapped a glare at her, his face puffier than before and his eyes paler. "I made this whole world so I could find a girl who'd, y'know, get it! But did you? No!"

Everything around her felt as slippery as she imagined an icy sidewalk would. "Then this isn't... real?"

"Duh!" He waved an arm, and he seemed to be shorter now, too. "I took all the fantasy clichés you girls like and pumped them into a talking animal world so we'd be the only two real people! Then we'd have adventures fighting the bad guy, fall in love, and end up together forever!" He aimed his scowl at Princess Margo and her family. "But you haven't even been here twelve hours, and you've already solved the puzzle!"

"Puzzle?" Parts of Sarah's brain seemed to be slowly rumbling back to life. "But...how? How could you make—?"

"A genie." Jim snapped his fingers, and Haxon came drifting over, the hedgehog melting the closer he got till he looked more like a frowning little rain cloud than anything else. "I found this clay jar in my uncle's basement when I inherited his house, and when Hax came out, I knew right away what was happening. So I told him I'd set him free as soon as he found the right girl for me, a girl who had a good head on her and knew what stuff was really important." He rubbed his chin. "Which I guess *is* you, the way you figured it out so quick. The others sure never made it this far."

More parts of Sarah's brain pricked up. "Others?"

Jim waved his hand again. "We've had, what, nine or ten we've run through?" He sighed. "Some of 'em were pretty good, but they all got killed in attacks and traps and stuff I set up along the way." The hard glint in his eye made Sarah's throat go dry. "So whaddaya think, Hax? Maybe wipe her memory and run her through again?"

"Master," the cloud said with Haxon's voice, Cockney accent and all, "your wish was to find a girl who would 'get it.'" Arms pulled away from the cloud's sides, hands on the ends that made air quotes when he spoke those last two words. "Well, this one got it better'n *you* did. So how 'bout we all get on with the 'happily ever after,' huh?" He did the air quotes again. "After you wish me free, I mean."

The rude noise Jim made with his lips didn't startle Sarah at all. "Like *that* was ever gonna happen," he said.

Haxon shrank visibly even though he was still only about a foot and a half tall.

"Nope," Jim went on. He reached into the folds of his robe and pulled out something about the size of a measuring cup, off-white and ceramic with a little lid covering the top. "Let's start it over again, but she's like the animals and doesn't remember any of it." He frowned. "This'd be so much easier if you could just make one of them fall in love with me..."

Sarah snapped fully awake for the first time in minutes, connections sparking through her. "*You're* the villain!" She raised her left fist so the diamonds of her great-aunt's ring were pointing at him. "I'm here to defeat you by the power of everything that's good in the universe!"

Jim blinked at her. "What the Hell are you talking about?" He gestured to the throne room. "This is *my* universe, babe. I'm the only one who says what happens here."

Unable to stop a sneer—and not really wanting to, either—Sarah shook her head. "You're a tyrant and a coward and a murderer, and if the rules of magic work anything like they do in the stories, then you—"

"Whoa!" He actually took a step back from her. "Murderer? I never killed anyone!"

"Those other 'girls.'" Sarah wanted to make her own air quotes around the word, but that might upset the ring's aim. "If your genie can't make people fall in love, then he can't kill people and can't bring them back from the dead either! So everyone you said died here: what happened to them, huh?"

A twitch jerked across Jim's face. "No one really died! It's...it's like a video game, right?" He snapped his head around to look at Haxon. "Right?"

The cloud sagged. "I explained this to you after you presented me with the rough draft of your wish, master. The traps you had me construct contained a possibility of proving lethal, and my genie powers couldn't prevent that lethality since I was working from your designs." He shrugged. "You wish for an axe, I give you an axe. What you do with it then's entirely up to you."

Jim's twitch seemed to have settled in just below his left eye, his gaze focused on Sarah's outstretched fist where the ring was growing warm against her finger.

"So," Sarah said, part of her unsure what to do while the other part had never been more sure, "since you *are* a tyrant and a coward and a murderer, I banish you from this, your former realm, and turn you over to the universe." Little bolts of lightning began sparking around her hand, then it shot out to surround him. "But you'll be leaving Haxon's jar when you go."

"No!" Jim struggled against the jagged cords

of lightning. "It was Haxon! He tricked me! I...I didn't know...didn't know what he meant! This is all his fault!" The streams of lightning thickened and brightened: squinting, Sarah watched them form a gigantic hand, its fingers and thumb squeezing Jim tighter. "No!" he shouted again, but then the blue and crackling hand shot upward, carrying him with it through the vaulted stone ceiling without leaving a mark.

Sarah's ears popped, and the silence crashed back into place...except for a tiny grinding like stone against stone. Something was wobbling on the floor, and she caught her breath to see that it was the little ceramic jar Jim had been holding.

The silence somehow deepened, but Sarah pushed her gaze away from the jar to the little cloud.

He'd changed back to a hedgehog again, his Zorro outfit now a red vest and fez. "Funny," he said, not looking at her, "how you mentioned you had your three wishes worked out, isn't it?"

Sarah swallowed. "Is this one of those stories where the person wishing the genie free has to take the genie's place in the bottle?" She held up her hand. "No, wait! It doesn't matter!" Lunging forward, she dropped to her knees, grabbed the jar, and said, "I wish Haxon was free to make his own choices!"

"Damn it, Sarah!" Little paws grabbed her wrists, and she found herself looking directly into Haxon's face, his snout and forehead wrinkled. "If I'd been wunna them real criminal genies that got us all imprisoned and enslaved to begin with—"

"But you're not." She cocked her head and decided that she'd better double check. "Are you?"

"No!" He let go of her hands and folded his arms. "But you had no way of knowing that!"

She had to laugh. "I had no way of knowing *anything!* I mean, every story's a little bit different, right?"

How the whole frozen room got even quieter, Sarah had no idea. But it did, Haxon's angry expression slowly smoothing and stretching into wide-eyed astonishment. "I...I can *feel* it. You wished me free without taking a single thing for yourself."

He just looked so cute, standing there dazed and confused, that Sarah almost leaned forward to hug him. But doing anything that might startle a hedgehog was a bad-enough idea; startling a hedgehog who was also a genie just seemed like a recipe for all kinds of unhappiness. So, in her least-startling tone—gentle and a little coaxing like she used on the kids who were nervous about getting their eyes dilated, she said, "I wouldn't mind getting a hug, if that'd be all right."

With a laugh of his own, he jumped forward, wrapped his arms around her, and the whole room burst back to life, Princess Margo's voice above all the other shouts and cheers, crying, "Mama! Papa! Inigo! I've missed you so, so much!"

"Thank you," Haxon was murmuring into Sarah's ear. "You've saved me—saved everybody here, really—from that jerkwad using us over and over again in his weird little dating game."

Sarah put some more pieces together. "He forced you to create this world, so it's all real, right? Like you said, a cliché, but a *living* cliché..."

She felt him nod, soft bristles brushing the side of her neck. "Less of a cliché, now, with Jimmy not around to force me into remaking things the way he wanted."

"Then—" Sarah started, but Pidge's voice burst over her:

"Hey!" The hummingbird's familiar colorful flashes went off in Sarah's peripheral vision, first on her right, then on her left, then on her right again. "Where's Godfrey? He was right here a minute ago, wasn't he?"

Haxon went very still in Sarah's embrace, and she swallowed. "Godfrey's gone," she said, gently pushing Haxon away so she could stand. Pidge's voice had carried, of course, so nearly everyone was looking at the three of them. Sarah swallowed again and spread her arms. "He was the force behind Darkfang, actually, and was propping him up with some very powerful magic. That's the real reason I came: to defeat Godfrey. I...I just... I didn't know it till right now."

That led to gasps and cheers, and Sarah did her best to smile, thinking of the women who'd preceded her here.

They stayed in her thoughts, though, during the ceremony in which Princess Margo presented her with the title of Dame Sarah, Heroine of the Realm. "You'll always be welcome in Azuredale," the princess said, now wearing a frilly gown with more shades of green than Sarah thought there were names for. Sarah was down on one knee, her own gown a deep burgundy that felt softer than silk against her skin, and she bent her head so Princess Margo could reach far enough up to put a golden medallion on a silver chain around her neck.

"Thank you, Your Highness, Your Majesties." Sarah stood and bowed to the princess's parents on their thrones. "I hope to visit again when things have settled down a bit."

The banquet that night overflowed with food and music and dancing, but after an hour or so, Sarah slipped out a side door into the palace gardens. Down a moonlit path, she wasn't at all startled to find Haxon in his red vest waiting for her. "Will I?" she asked. "Be able to visit again, I mean?"

He smiled. "Whadda your books and cartoons say?"

She waggled a hand from side to side. "The record's mixed. But I'd like to, if you wouldn't mind."

"It'd be my pleasure." He bowed to her. "I knew it when I first sensed you: genre-savvy, sure, but unlike Jimmy, you felt the real power of these stories, heard what they were trying to say, learned what they were trying to teach. You didn't think anything like this'd ever happen to you, but you gave it all a place in your heart anyway so you were ready when it did." Brushing at his vest with one paw, he waved the other at the palace. "And now that Jimmy's not making me rewind everything, I can't wait to see what develops 'round here."

"Yeah." Sarah had to clear her throat. "But...the others Jim brought here before me. Could I have a list, please? I know there's nothing I can do, but—" She shrugged. "They had families and friends, and maybe...I don't know..."

More than a little sadness tinged Haxon's smile; he flicked his claws and pulled a small notebook out of the air. "You're a good person, Sarah." Blue sparks danced around his paws, and Sarah felt the air tingling. "Anytime you wanna visit, you call my name into your ring, and I'll pop on over to pick you up." The light and sounds of the party on the other side of the trees between her and the palace faded to darkness and silence. The chill of November replaced the previous warmth, and she glanced around at the park she knew so well.

Colorful specks caught her attention, puffing away from the diamonds of her ring, and she blinked at the notebook she was holding. Nothing like *this* ever happened in the cartoons. But, well, life wasn't a cartoon, was it?

With a sad smile of her own, she started back down the path toward home.

Michael H. Payne's novels have been published by Tor Books and Sofawolf Press while his short stories have appeared in places like *Asimov's SF*, the *Zooscape* website, and 11 of the last 12 *Sword & Sorceress* anthologies. His poetry shows up in *Star*Line*, various Rhysling Award anthologies, and the *Silver Blade* website, and he updates his two webcomics, *Daily Grind* and *Terebinth*, at a rate of four pages a week. Please feel free to consult hyniof.com for more information.

Join us on Facebook for updates, news and announcements.

www.facebook.com/spaceandtimemagazine

AUTHORTUNITIES.

Exercise your writes.
Get published.
Make change.

A weekly calendar of author opportunities for busy writers who need to know who, how much and when is the deadline.

authortunities.substack.com

Magic Mushroom

Written by **Sam Crain**
Illustrated by Arthur Haywood

Pestalotiopsis microspora. The little Amazonian fungus had to be researched thoroughly even as the world (and its cetaceans) choked with need. The pachyderms were long gone by then. But the scientists craved certainty and tested each hypothesis. And biologists, mycologists, biochemists, and their assorted graduate students worked in climate-controlled domes, consuming a practical *sea* of agar as they taught themselves how to farm the fungi. In those years, robot bees and pollination by drone kept the world from starving itself, even as starvation threatened to become the world's main crop.

Jermaine was among the mycologists. The initial tests and experiments had begun just as he was entering grad school, so he'd gotten his Master's and joined the Dutch lab experimenting on different strains of plastic-eating fungi, his PhD dissertation detailing their evolving testing procedures. Sleeping his four hours a night, he grinned: *actually saving the world* was his research—helping to, anyway. Lunchtimes, he'd read emails from his best friend and undergrad roommate Alex, who put Jermaine to shame idealistically. Alex had gone into Philosophy and History, their late-night talks about ethics and morality having kept Jermaine from going into Petrochemicals when he'd declared a specialty. Alex would have sighed but said nothing.

Alex'd landed an adjunct job, and Jermaine worried they were approaching burn-out, between research *and* reaching students. Low enrollments. *I don't know how to talk about ethics, and neither do they. It ends up word salad. But—*

But knowledge without ethics is worse than useless, Jermaine finished from memory.

The first photo of a black hole, the first time someone broke the sound barrier—these were climactic moments. The Day of the Mushroom was subdued: five flutes of hoarded champagne, toasting their project director Emile. Emile had bowed, toasting them back. "The fungus—our dear little mushroom—eats plastic, *and* we can grow it. It is a beginning," he said in accented English.

That champagne had popped along Jermaine's tongue and he'd itched to write the news to Alex. But the research was proprietary, and UnCorp, the major tech company that funded them, was strict in monitoring external communication. Deals with devils, indeed.

But they'd done it.

He'd gone back to his desk to run some numbers, maybe get a jump on writing the report and the SOP for culturing the fungi. No time to waste.

Emile had followed. "Jermaine, there you are. You've been my right hand in all this."

"It's been a pleasure." He looked up from his screen.

"The board of directors want to meet with us to discuss the *next step*," said Emile. "Now. Will you come upstairs?"

Jermaine had gone, straightening his clothes as he

went. He'd always hated talking to the money—even when they cut fat checks.

"Good, the lab coats are here"—by way of greeting. "We can get started."

The man at the head of the long table commanded the room, eyes shiny above a dark blue power tie. He was angular more than slender. "I understand you've had a success," he said.

"That is right." Emile beamed.

"I'm delighted. You can grow the plastic-eating mushroom after all?"

"The initial strain consumes plastic outright, and we can grow it. That is correct."

"The later strains?"

"We are still working on those," Emile said. "We'll know more in a few months."

Jermaine stole a look at his boss, who was *lying* outright. They *knew* about the miracle of the second strain. Mouth shut and eyes down, Jermaine.

"Well, we'll get started with Strain A at least. It'll whet everyone's appetite."

"Yes," Jermaine said. "We can eliminate large landfills—even start actually efficient recycling centers and community waste clean-ups—" No more wishful recycling, he thought, rinsing plastic tubs and *hoping*, no more transporting waste overseas—

"Easy, kid." The CEO was smiling, but it just didn't touch those shiny eyes. "Think of the administrative costs. The logistics. And I'd say UnCorp deserves something for its trouble." Murmurs of agreement then, even Jermaine nodded as UnCorp's CEO's gaze bored into his, sick with understanding: UnCorp meant to capitalize on his team's discovery. Profits would be made.

He opened his mouth to object, feeling Alex's righteous anger searing his own insides, but Emile kicked him hard under the table, upsetting his water glass.

"So sorry," Emile said. "Excuse us, please. Tests to run, you understand."

"Of course." The CEO's heartiness was like cold, generic canned soup: over-concentrated and practically fake.

Emile took Jermaine in hand. "Young fool. You could have ruined everything." He spoke directly into Jermaine's ear.

"But—" Jermaine's ankle was still smarting.

"*Non*. Listen. UnCorp will sell this *mushroom* to those who can pay."

"But—the countries that can't—They need the fungus most."

"That's what I am saying to you. Now. You will take Type B with you. You've been accepted to a postdoc in Nigeria. Congratulations."

Realization was dawning grey in Jermaine's mind.

"I will miss you of course. And I hear rumors you will be in high demand at labs in Malaysia, the Philippines, and Indonesia soon after. So work hard, yes?" All this Emile said in the barest of whispers. His eyes were bright and softened by tears. "You leave today. *Au revoir*."

On a plane to Cairo. Regional transport would take him further, but Emile had warned against flying directly to his destination. "Guard Type B with your life" had been Emile's farewell. Not a cliché, this time. Tucked up against the tiny window, he wrote a letter to Alex, a goodbye, just in case, fairly owed—and more. *I love you.* He'd nearly scribbled it out, sealed the envelope before he lost his nerve.

The spores for growing Type B were tucked inside his sock, its capsule small enough to swallow if necessary.

It dug against his leg over every bump in the road from Al Minya to Aswan, driving within sight of the Nile. A local named Muhammed had met him there. "Fly over Sudan, not drive through," he'd explained. "Next stop is N'Djamena, long as our fuel holds out."

Jermaine nodded, thinking of the letter he'd sent. *This* was worth the risk. Surreal, how much depended on the capsule down his sock, UnCorp's most valuable asset. Harder to worry that UnCorp would be after him, in the African sky. A company that owned most of the Western world's entertainment industry wanted to geometrically grow its fortune with a magic mushroom.

"We'll refuel here, but stay close to me. And put that on." Muhammed tossed him a robe and a head covering. "It's a Boubou. Keep your mouth shut and you might pass long enough for us to get in the air."

"My father is from Ghana."

"Yes, I can read him in your face. *Definitely* do not speak."

Jermaine kept close to the plane. The Boubou's cloth was smooth over his arms, and colorful.

Muhammed was back almost before Jermaine missed him, holding what looked like a bottle of vegetable oil.

"Ginger beer." He passed it over.

Its flavor was sharper than champagne as they flew over Eastern Nigeria. Jermaine was dozing when they landed.

"Welcome to Abuja."

He'd made it. He and the Type B both. "Thanks."

Kala remembered when the mushrooms came, three of them in a sealed plastic sphere. She'd been hard at work with her mother, planting saved seeds. The earth went deep under her nails, and they'd finally finished, to find a man waiting for them. This black man in his white coat had pressed the sphere into her mother's hand and told her to plant it in their rubbish heap. It would help them, he'd promised. Mother had thought the white-coated man was crazy, but she'd done it. It couldn't hurt, she'd said. They'd wanted to invite the man in for a drink of water, at least, but he'd shaken his head, saying he had more people still to see. His speech had been halting, not local. Kala had wrinkled up her nose and laughed: even she had been able to tell that.

It had been a month, or a bit more, and Kala had gone out to the rubbish heap and found mushrooms where their plastic trash had been—mushrooms the man assured her family were safe to eat. She'd run to tell Mother that the man—Jermaine, he'd called himself—had been right.

In the days and months to come, the profusion of mushrooms stimulated Mother's ingenuity for cooking. They were fried, stewed, dried, boiled, roasted. The rubbish heaps shrank in time, and the edge of Kala's hunger was blunted as she watched the seeds they'd planted on Mushroom Day grow green fingers from the earth. She spent long hours standing guard over both plots though Mother said there was no need to guard the mushrooms—the man Jermaine had brought a few to every family in their village, and the next one over. Even so, Kala watched, eyes narrowed against the bright sun above her head.

Sam Crain lives in Fremont, CA. Now that she's finished her PhD in English, she's free to return to her first love, writing stories, which she does whenever she can steal her pens back from her cats. Two of her stories can both be found on Mythic Beast Studios. Her flash fiction Tacit was just released by *Does it Have Pockets*, and brand-new flash fictions Hephaestus and Unsanctioned Transfiguration are forthcoming in *Aôthen Magazine* and the anthology *Borne in the Blood*.

MAXWELL I. GOLD

BLEEDING RAINBOWS AND OTHER BROKEN SPECTRUMS

A lurid poetic journey explored through the eyes of the gay sexual experience.

PREORDER NOW
COMING PRIDE 2023
HEXPUBLISHERS.COM

INTRODUCTION BY
ANGELA YURIKO SMITH

Blood and Space

Written by C. H. Williams
Illustrated by Angela Yuriko Smith

I am the first vampire in space. BSc PHD, a doctor of science and a lover of stars. They wanted a satellite engineer, and with three-hundred years of knowledge, I'm the very best. All I asked was for good company, and a healthy supply of blood.

They sent me a donor. I feed to live. He lives to feed. He maintains the outside structure and I remain in the artificial light. In a solar powered vessel I am indebted to the only force which threatens my kind.

We pass the time playing cards. Not all vampires are into blood sports.

C. H. Williams resides in the Welsh mountains with her nerdy husband, and their wonderful daughter, along with a growing collection of rocks, sticks, and feathers from their adventures together.

This is What I Am (I Sing of Revolution)
Felicia Martínez

I am not a rose.
I am not a sunflower following sunlight stuck in rhythms.
This is ignoring moonshine.

Nor am I a butterfly predictably changing like the earthworm's slow
story. She never asks for wings.
Do you hear me? No, I am not of the garden at all
cultivated and paid for with the bodies of deep change. Unfathomable.

Their loss is also the uncertainty of me. I am the pollen's reach replete
with threadbare seeds. I am the dog lapping chlorophyll
from a dying sea. I sing.
Like all futures.

Is it this you will not believe?
Then I hear you. Sometimes all I hear
is you even when there are other beats rising in the mud and muck of me.

I push my hands in deep, I squelch and pat and pull until patterns
so fundamental raise my grooves, my gritty membranes into
forms I recognize at last. Like rain.
This is beauty.

I'll ask you again. When did you forget that the sky's sorrow is my life, too?
That it wasn't by my power that you fell hopeless and broken,
not by these worn hands

these shattered mandibles that clack and shiver and
still shelter our salted planet, this strangled sky.
I hold them all
like a seeded star. Just listen.

I am the fish
I am the amoeba
I am the small sparrow with the lizard inside
that walked once like thunder and may again.
That's how this works. Didn't you know? So don't you dare say to me,

"Who asked the whale to walk on land?" as if your existence
didn't require things braver than you and more willing to rise up for their limbs
and their wings and their homes and their hope.

That's the pattern. And the song. Known by every lasting future
every crack and howl
in throats that fill with endless shimmering skies.

And we are joy.

We scuttle
we dance and we fly
and we are this earth too.

The Shepherd's Enantiodromia
J. S. Graham

A Digital Mystery Play
(and comment on prolepsis)

That's not really what this is about.
This is about seeing things.
Things people say don't exist.
I saw my father—
perched upon an oak in Chesterfield.
Laughing in his death clothes.

Cathected—roam
[you]
Souls in flight past silicon shores
Pulling wool over the eyes
of the sweet goddess of sleep

At the Edge of the World, There Were No Gods
Maxwell I. Gold

Drawn by some ravenous and wicked breath, surreptitious utterances whispered beneath cracked stone in crumbling temples; the slaughter of old gods and monsters. Useless monuments thrown into the broken and beleaguered seas where no tremulous songs could be heard, and only the naïve mutilations wrought by a heinous and discerning world continued without cause or resistance. Indigent and depraved were the epic tales, mad armies wrought by bloodlust and unspeakable power smashed against the tried, beaten corpse of the earth. Titans they may have been, worshipped by the hairless parasites and soft-pink tissue sacs, soon discarded like ashen snowflakes tumbling from some swollen mushroom cloud.

Ennobled marble flecks like flower petals, withered away beneath the new and despicable machinations of plastic, metal sinews which rose above old mythologies, reshaping them into something truly unknowable. A solution committed without recompense, these gods were soon banished through the faceless and reckless dirges beyond time until at the end of the world there remained no reflection or revelation; and sapien ghouls wandered the lonely, desolate world.

The Troll
Michael Bacchia

Feeling terror in the unknown reaches of space,
There are many deaths in this unforgiving place,
As one nears the gravitational pull of a black hole,
It is there that sits the troll,
To whom a toll must be paid,
Around which lethal satelites are arrayed,
In the blackness lie the floating dead,
Their engines not fast enough to get away,
A graveyard of space ships that refused to pay.

Solar System Real Estate
Casey Aimer

Don't tell me that living on the moon
or some far-flung celestial sphere
will unravel me for the better.

My existence stays the same
despite changing scenery.
So stop howling for this
human to try new spaces.
Shifting pace doesn't bring
perspective, only reproduces
extended homesick alienation.

Let's unsnarl ourselves here first,
start frowning at the consequences
of planet-sized fences and showcase
alternative differences to worldviews
like white picket planets painted black
with polychromatic and bioluminescent
paint slathered haphazardly atop each peak.

Her Father's Daughter

Written by **Spencer Sekulin**
Illustrated by Mark Levine

Iseula Aoyama felt her eyes glaze over as she stared at the distorted mess of the *Inari's* holographic sensory output. The smell of strong coffee, and its bitter aftertaste, didn't compensate for thirty wakeless hours—but how could she sleep, knowing what waited out there?

Or not out there. This could be a waste of time and fuel.

To her surprise, her heart fluttered at the prospect. Better than what she'd come for.

The sensory output rippled, followed by a beep from the proximeter.

Iseula jolted up in her reclined pilot's seat and slapped the empty coffee pods off the nav console. She squinted through the junk-encrusted orbit of Azeroth II, ignoring the plethora of old satellites, focusing on the tiny red indicator dot that had popped up on her HUD. Maybe the irradiated planet's azure glow was playing tricks on her eyes. She'd been getting false echoes for days. But when the knot in her stomach turned into nausea, she knew she'd found it—and *him*—after eight long years.

The man who'd shattered her heart.

Hands trembling, Iseula dialed down the engines until she barely felt the vibrations, then held her breath as she eased closer. Leftover from the Andromeda-Solarian war, Azeroth II was an odd planet. It had two debris rings, each going opposite directions, gravitational anomalies creating a countercurrent, a bi-directional orbit that turned the zone between into a garburator.

Her target lurked right on the edge.

Debris squealed against the *Inari's* hull, but years of dishonest salvage work had left her ugly as sin anyway, and in Null Space a pristine ship made you a target. Iseula's sleep-mucked eyes burned the longer they stared; weeks of failure, months of false leads, and years of clawing doubt piling on with every click of the proximity gauge. The red dot turned into a blob, then the blocky length of a rusted ship wedged between two dead satellites.

An old Fuanang light freighter. Iseula bit her lip.

Could be one of a thousand. Maybe I'm wrong.

Yet when she read the name scrawled along its side, she pinched the skin between her eyebrows. The *Melpomene*. Dad's ship. Just what she'd hoped for. Just what she'd feared.

"Dammit," she whispered. "Why'd I have to find you?"

Iseula closed her eyes and counted to ten, reaching out to feel the threadbare rabbit doll strapped into her co-pilot's seat, garnering a fraction of the comfort it had given her as a child. Then she flipped the safety cover off the weapons control, thumb poised to unleash a burst of explosive shells. She simultaneously dialed in a local transmission, counting on the planet's radiation to distort her voice.

Space and Time

"Inari to Melpomene, what's your status?"

Nothing. Not even static.

Iseula waited, thumb aching, heart pounding. "Dad... it's Iseula. You there? I just... wanted to talk about it." She swallowed hard. "We can *talk*."

Still nothing. Iseula grated her teeth, feeling eight years pile on her thumb. She burned to press that trigger... yet she found herself bringing the *Inari* alongside to couple with the *Melpomene's* portside tether instead. A shudder rattled the deck, followed by a groan of clamps and the hiss of pressure equalization. The move would disturb their orbit, and the *Inari's* autopilot would only keep them out of the planet's countercurrent until one of its daily glitches. She would have to do this quickly. Iseula met the doll's glassy stare. "Hold down the fort. This... won't take long."

Childhood memories replied—of Mom holding that doll, miming as she read bedtime stories. Iseula smirked and stepped into the tight corridor. Crazy for someone in her early twenties to have a doll. But this was Null Space. Everyone was crazy.

And out for revenge.

Her antimatter pistol waited on its hook. She reached for it, then hesitated.

This isn't right... but things haven't been right for a long time, have they?

She took the weapon, rubbing its textured grip as she went to the airlock. After donning her scarred EVA suit, she looked at her helmet and her reflection in the visor. Those hazel eyes. That pale, rounded face. That void-black hair. Dad through and through. She donned the helmet with a pressurizing hiss, painfully aware of what she was doing.

Mom wouldn't approve. Mom had believed in forgiveness.

"I have to find out," Iseula whispered. "I need to know why you had to die. Why Dad abandoned us. Abandoned *you*. You can't blame me for that. No one can."

She cracked the airlock's seal and jumped into the zero-g tether linking the ships, paying a bitter glance through the portholes at Azeroth II's war-scarred surface. Another dead planet left in humanity's wake, like the lives of many good people she'd known. A chime sounded in her earpiece—another echo on the sensors. Tingles crept up her spine. What if there was something to those echoes after all?

All the more reason to make this quick.

The *Melpomene's* rusted airlock wouldn't open, but Iseula hadn't intended to knock. She jammed her pistol against its mechanism and blasted through with a crackling burst of antimatter. Dusty air wafted out, specks of debris tinkling against her visor. She eyed her HUD readouts. No lights. Only auxiliary systems and life support—and far too much carbon dioxide for an uninhabited ship.

Now to find the man who'd left her entire colony for dead.

Fresh boot marks marred the dusty floor. Iseula followed.

She swallowed hard as she crept through corridors, headlamp banishing the dark but not the memories—of all the times she'd been aboard, back when she'd dreamed of being a merchant like Dad. The engineering compartment she'd tinkered in for hours. The tight crew quarters she'd made pillow forts in. The echo of laughter down those narrow metal hallways. Good memories.

War changed a lot of things. Changed people, too.

Cheating on Mom had been bad enough. Running away while a pandemic ravaged their home, with the only ship they might have used to escape, had driven a hot spike through Iseula's heart that she still couldn't get out.

The footprints led to the bridge. Iseula thumbed her pistol's trigger guard.

Please don't be there, a voice in her head whispered.

Please be there, hissed another.

Iseula burst into the control room, sweeping her lamp in a silver arc. Nothing but swirls of dust and empty chairs and dead screens. She muttered a curse and followed the footprints towards the only chair turned away—the tall-backed captain's seat. It was sagging to the right, weighted by something. Or someone. Iseula's heart drummed in her ears. She turned the seat. A small box sat there instead, sealed with pipe tape, a hole cut in the side facing her.

A red light blinked on.

Oh sh—! The explosion threw Iseula across the room. She flipped over the navigation console and cartwheeled into the wall. Her vision swam, her ears rang, but she still saw a shadow detach from a roof vent. Iseula aimed wildly, lighting up the room with crackling red shots. The shadow darted into the corridor.

Iseula staggered to her feet, coughing. Shrapnel riddled her EVA suit's chest plate. *He almost killed me.* Tears of rage stung her eyes as she pursued.

Her attacker ran down the corridor, taking a left at the first junction. Iseula knew she wasn't fast enough in her suit, but she knew every shortcut. Blasting a hatch, she ducked into a maintenance corridor—and glimpsed another red light in an alcove. She dove forward. The blast rattled her brain and stung her back with heat. She staggered into the next hallway, cursing, and aimed as the shadow burst around the corner. The lamplight revealed blue eyes and a brown, freckled face. Iseula hesitated.

A kid?

The boy leapt through an open door, which groaned shut thereafter. The rec rooms. Iseula pounded against it, and when it didn't open, she blasted its lock into a molten wreck. Grunting, she shoved it open, aiming inside.

"All right, don't—!"

At least two dozen faces stared back, all wide-eyed and terrified. Children in tattered clothes and thin as sticks. The tables and chairs had been pushed aside to make space. Many lay under blankets, shivering and pale, while a few looked caught in the process of tending to them. Even with her helmet on, Iseula smelled the thick, sour air. By the stars, it smelled just like the pandemic-ridden infirmaries back home on Unschuld. A girl no older than eight dropped a cup, spilling water across the deck.

Iseula blinked. "What the hell is this?"

Someone whimpered, and another started crying.

"I..." Iseula realized she was still aiming. She lowered the weapon, sick to her stomach.

"Don't move," growled a voice.

The boy stood on her right, brandishing an old plasma cutter. Blue eyes, sandy hair, tanned skin with ashen freckles. Fourteen at most, but he primed the cutter as well as any adult, filling the room with its humming sapphire glow.

"Drop the gun," he said, voice shaking.

Iseula frowned. "Let's talk—"

"Drop it!"

"And if I don't?"

"I'll..." The boy set his jaw, working himself up for it. "I won't let you hurt them."

Iseula slowly angled herself towards him. "I'm not here to hurt anyone. I didn't even know you were here. I should be the one asking." She dropped her pistol and grabbed his wrist, narrowly avoiding losing her hand to the cutter, and slammed him against the wall. "What the hell are you doing on my father's ship and why did you just try to kill me?!"

The boy sputtered. "I thought you were with them!"

"Who's *them*?" Iseula heard more sobs from the others. It made her feel terrible. "Be more specific."

"V-Valefar's men."

Valefar? Iseula frowned. Where had she heard that before? She sighed and let him go, keeping her pistol ready. "Looks like we were both expecting someone else. What's your name?"

The boy stepped back, rubbing his wrist. "Aster."

"What's going on here?"

"We're... hiding."

"And how's that going? Half of you look sick as death."

Aster winced, color returning to his face. "We were on an evac pod, but it was marked. We didn't have anywhere else to go. It's... a long story."

Aren't they all? Iseula prepared another cutting remark, then stopped herself. It wasn't fair to them, whoever they were. Instead, she counted the children. Thirty, half sick. Most looked younger than ten. *And I was thinking of blowing this ship up. God, I almost did.* Her stomach lurched, and the sight of the nearest sick child, whose purpuric rash reached all the way to his forehead, finished the job. She stumbled into the corridor, throat on fire with bile as similar memories poured through her head.

"Are you okay?" Aster asked, watchful behind her.

Iseula tore off her helmet, taking deep breaths. "Fine. Just... confused. Was there anyone when you got here?"

"No."

Iseula flinched. So that was it. Dad wasn't even here. Had he ditched it years ago? Was he on some tropical world, living it up with another fling? There had to be a way to find out... A tremor shook the floor, followed by a deep groan—and an alert in Iseula's earpiece. The *Inari's* sensors were going wild.

"Stay right there," she told Aster.

Aster kept pace anyway. He didn't ask what was

happening. The look on his face told her he already knew.

The bridge basked in Azeroth II's azure glow. Beyond the dusty, ice-laced window loomed a large, wedge-shaped vessel painted in mottled greys. Iseula had seen many like it—the war between the Solarian Republic and the Andromeda Regenate had torn the neutral colonies apart. But this Regenate warship lacked the usual markings, its bow adorned with a snarling lion dashed with slashes of crimson.

Captain Elias Valefar. The name sprang through her mind like a bullet, dusted off from all the days spent drinking cheap booze at backwater stations. A decorated Regenate captain turned war criminal. How could she have forgotten? Her skin crawled as she watched three transports detach from the warship's ventral hangar. Suddenly all the echoes made sense.

He was stalking me all week, and I led him right to them.

Iseula glanced at Aster, but instead of terror, his face was set with grim determination.

I should run.

Her legs trembled to do just that. What did she owe these squatters? She'd lost count of how many times she'd ignored distress signals. How was this any different? Ever since she'd escaped her home planet, ever since she'd stolen the *Inari* from a drunk captain on a remote mining colony, her to-do list had always started with three words: don't die yet.

Another tremor shook the floor, followed by an echo of boarding craft cutting the hull. Acrid smoke crept from one of the air vents. Iseula found herself staring at Dad's seat, remembering his smile, his booming laughter… and the hurt of it all, twisting between her ribs like a hot knife. Running away was exactly what she hated him for, and here she was, about to rip a page from his book.

Iseula grabbed Aster by the arm and ran.

"Hey what—?"

"Aster, how well do you know this ship?"

"M-Most of it."

"Not enough. They'll find you in minutes." Iseula looked into his owlish blue eyes. "Lucky for you, I grew up here."

Aster grimaced. "Why are you helping us?"

"After you nearly blew me to bits?" Iseula shrugged. "When I find out, I'll let you know."

Thump. Thump. Thump.

Iseula held her breath and resisted the urge to scratch at the sweat trickling down her brow. Those footfalls were heavy. A full shock team in armored EVA suits. Suicide to fight against. Suicide to flee from. Almost suicide to hide from, too. She rubbed her pistol's trigger guard as she counted the pairs of boots passing over their hiding place.

She stopped counting at twenty.

Someone started sniffling.

"Keep them quiet," Iseula hissed.

Aster comforted a little girl who quivered beneath her threadbare sheets. The smell of sickness was overpowering. Everyone was cramped into a crawlspace between the ship's two levels, a gap left by the superstructure, accessible by a section of loosened deck. Four feet high, stretching from port to starboard, lit by emergency lamps. In her childhood she'd used it to play hide and seek. Funny how things came full circle.

"I think they're gone," Eviya whispered, the only one Aster's age, a pretty girl with ebony skin and auburn hair.

Iseula waited, hearing no more boots. She wanted to say they'd be safe, that Azeroth II's radiation would distort scans, but who was she kidding? The ghost of inevitability itched at the back of her mind.

"We can't stay here long," Aster whispered. "We left our food and water."

"We won't," Iseula said.

"Do you have an idea?"

No. Iseula glanced at all the malnourished faces. "We need to wait a little longer. They'll start digging through the cargo bays first."

Aster blinked. "Those are at the rear. You docked near the front."

Smart kid. "How about that long story? I'd like to know what I'm up against."

"I…" Aster's face scrunched up. He glanced at Eviya. Whatever passed between them made up his mind. "Our people were trying to escape the colonies. Valefar raided our ships, killed the adults, and took us to…" His face turned a greenish hue. "Sell."

Iseula wasn't surprised. Human trafficking had boomed after the war. "I'm sorry."

Aster nodded, already checking on the sick. Iseula found herself going with him, helping distribute what meager water they had—and battling memories she wanted to forget. The purple blotches on their skin, the desquamating rash, and that thick, hay-like odor. Mom's voice, withered like sandpaper…

"How did you escape?" Iseula asked, distracting herself.

"We tricked them." Aster paused, then shrugged. "I found a few holes in their security. Took one of their escape pods. I knew it would be traced, but then we found this ship, so we switched over and blew the pod. I hoped they'd think we drifted into the countercurrent."

"You know quite a lot for a kid. Those bombs were no joke."

Aster's lips quirked. "My dad captained a patrol vessel. Took me on as an apprentice." He swallowed, blinking rapidly. "I learned a lot from him."

Iseula nodded, wondering what it was like to have a father like that—one you could *trust*—and to lose him. Another tremor shook the floor, punctuated by a deep metallic groan. Iseula clicked her tongue. "More boarding craft."

"Y-Yeah." Aster took a shaky breath.

"Too many. You're telling me Valefar's going through all this trouble chasing a few scrawny kids into a hazardous debris field?"

Aster stiffened.

Knew it. Iseula grabbed his arm. "What did you do?"

"I… took something from him."

"What?"

Once more Aster glanced at Eviya. Once more, that silent conversation. At last, Eviya scooted over to a bundle of rags and pulled something out. A silvery metal sphere the size of a melon. Aster took it, grimacing. It had a small interface for security clearance, and gave off a staticky aura. A containment capsule. Military grade. Iseula's skin crawled just looking at it. What the hell had she gotten herself into?

"What's inside?"

"I don't know, but it looked important." Aster bit his lip. "I thought it would give us leverage if we got caught."

Iseula snorted. "You'd think your father would've taught you not to toy with the ambitions of dangerous men."

Eviya scowled. "We didn't know."

"No, she's right." Aster looked deflated. "This is my fault."

"You didn't know!" Eviya touched Aster's arm. "Don't listen to her. She's—"

"What?" Iseula growled. "An asshole?"

Eviya's furrowed eyebrows said as much. "What about you? Why are *you* here?"

Iseula felt her shoulders tense. She looked away, pretending to check her wrist computer, then actually doing so. The *Inari* was still docked, and no one had toyed with her systems. "I think we've waited enough. I'm taking my ship back."

Aster squared his bony shoulders. "I'll help you."

"No." Iseula was surprised how forcefully she said it. "Stay with them. Get everyone to the port side, ready to move. Once I'm certain my ship is safe, we'll need to go fast." She turned to leave, but Eviya caught her arm, her golden-brown eyes drilling into her.

"You're not lying, are you?"

"I…" Iseula felt her throat tighten. "No. I'm not that sort of person."

Am I?

Iseula winced with a dozen aches and sprains. Thirty minutes spent crawling through cramped vents would do that. She brushed another layer of dust off her visor and felt for the edges of the vent grating.

"Well?" a female voice said below.

Iseula froze.

"Lieutenant Cross," a man said, startled. "Nothing yet."

"Then search *harder*," grunted the woman. "Doesn't matter that scans are down. This ship's full of footprints and feces. Those brats are here, along with whoever was on that optical migraine of shitcan."

Iseula rolled her eyes. *Gee, thanks.*

The woman sighed. "We must find it. Doesn't matter the cost. Valefar's right, it's our only chance. Otherwise all of… *this*… was for nothing. Understood?"

"Yes, Ma'am."

"Good. Now search every inch of this junkheap!"

Iseula waited for the footsteps to fade, then eased

Space and Time

the vent off. All clear. The *Inari* was tethered down the hall, close enough to feel its idling vibrations. Iseula slipped her pistol out of its holster and took a deep breath. She dropped into the corridor in a cloud of dust—and saw a cigarette flare. A young woman in a battle-scarred EVA suit leaned against the wall a few feet away, helmet off, cigarette hanging forgotten from her lips as she gawked. Crew cut. Brown eyes. Lieutenant's stripes. That Cross lady. At the same instant another soldier stepped through a hatch.

Iseula's hand snapped up on its own, pistol barking. The second soldier dropped, and Cross dove forward, cigarette scattering embers on the deck. She swatted Iseula's arm aside, her own sidearm drawn and angling towards her jaw. Iseula jerked her head, shots screaming past her ear. They grappled, eye to eye, grunting and hissing, until they stumbled through an open door. Iseula glimpsed books on the floor, felt one trip her, and went down hard, pulling Cross with her.

More shots howled. Iseula didn't know if any hit. Didn't feel anything but a burning rush of terror and adrenaline. She found herself on her back, Cross's face inches away, eyes narrow and cold, the barrel of her pistol looming like a depthless void. Iseula drove her helmeted forehead upwards. The pistol glanced aside just before it fired, burning the top of Iseula's shoulder. Meanwhile her visor slammed into Cross's nose with a bloody crunch. Cross grunted and listed sideways, dazed. Iseula threw her off, grabbed her pistol, and shot her three times in the chest. Iseula staggered back, staring at the smoldering holes in the body's chest plate.

I just killed two people.

The thought hung around her like smoke. She retched.

I had to. I had no choice!

Her vision blurred. God, why cry now? She made out the books on the floor, the shelves, an old desk. Dad's study. Torn apart, shelves and drawers empty, everything strewn across the floor. How many hours had she spent here as a child, reading books beyond her understanding? How many times had Dad fallen asleep at that desk, halfway through penning his thoughts?

Doesn't matter. The Inari *is waiting, and more of those bastards are coming.*

A leatherbound journal lay on the desk, still open, coated in dust. The same journal she remembered, with a sapphire tassel to mark a page. She gently brushed the dust aside, knowing her father in every curl of blue ink—and seeing her name amidst it. Could it be? She set her pistol down and picked up the journal…

An antimatter charge flashed past her eyes, blasting the journal from her hands with a puff of atomized paper.

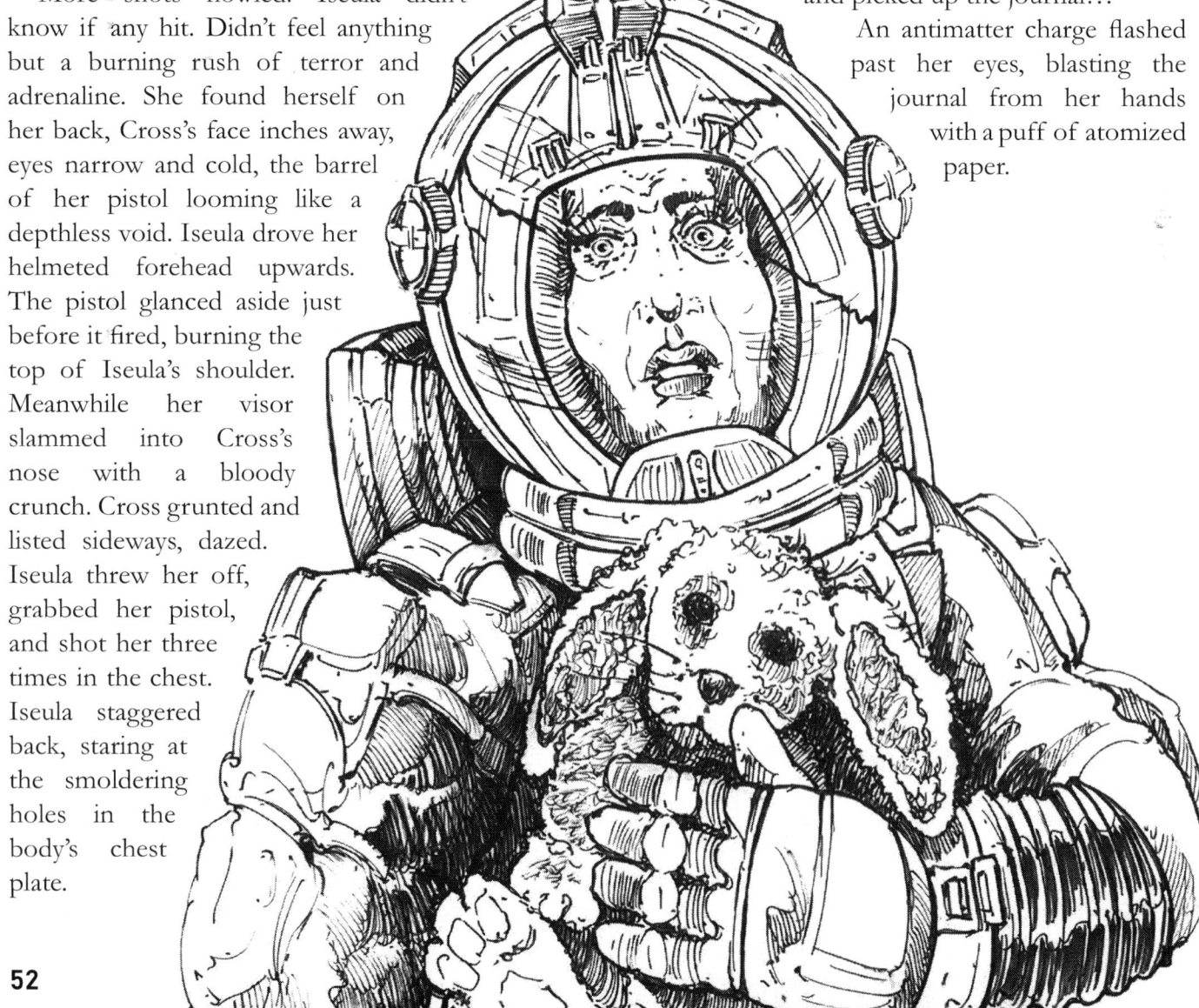

52

Cross stood, livid, the holes in her breastplate no longer smouldering, revealing a secondary layer beneath. "You're screwed." She took aim—and jolted, a loud *gong* sounding as something struck the back of her head. She dropped in a heap. Aster stood behind her, wielding a sizable fire extinguisher.

"I told you to stay up there!" Iseula said.

Aster dropped the extinguisher. "And how's that working for you?"

Iseula muttered a curse and grabbed her pistol along with pen and paper, then Cross's pistol, then dragged Aster into the corridor. Two low-powered shots melted the door's mechanism to keep Cross trapped. The corridor was still empty. A glance at the corpse gave her another taste of her morning coffee.

"Thank you," she said at last, taking out the pen.

Aster stole a nervous glance at the body. "What are you writing?"

"A backup. In case this goes sideways. There's a mothballed shuttle in the hangar. Wait till they've searched it, then get everyone onboard. I bet it still works. My father wasn't a lot of things… but he ran a tight ship." She handed Aster the note. "Pass this to Eviya, then keep an eye out. You see anything, you come to me. Got it?"

Aster grimaced. "What if there's more on your ship?"

"I'll deal with it." Iseula shoved the extra pistol into his hands. When he stared at it, she gripped his shoulder. "Just in case."

Aster nodded, stealing another glance at the corpse.

All right. Iseula ducked into her ship's tether. Her hands wouldn't stop shaking. It wasn't just the killing. The truth had been in Dad's journal. Now it was dust. She swallowed hard as she stalked through the *Inari's* tight corridors, but no one was aboard, and the cockpit was just as she'd left it. As usual, the rabbit's stoic silence left room for imagination.

"I'm late, I know," Iseula said. "Unexpected guests. And it's not my fault a bunch of shit magnets infested the place!" She jumped into her seat, flipping switches to prime the drive system—and froze when her hand gripped tether control. *Wait, what am I doing?* She stared into the azure expanse, seeing the distant, shadowy outline of the cruiser. This was her chance to escape. Her only chance. Then Iseula remembered the look on Eviya's face. The brittle hope, and the pensive doubt. A look she'd seen before.

When did I get like this? Iseula pulled her hand away. The girl she'd been wouldn't have even considered it. Like Mom, she'd have done the right thing, not what was convenient. Since when had she become a heartless drifter? By the stars, how much of herself had she thrown away these last eight years? *Am I really no different than—?*

A tremor shook the *Inari*. Something blotted out Azeroth II's glow, and Iseula found herself staring at the cannon-bristling nose of a Regenate gunship. She ducked as the first round punched through the window. She heard a blast and the howl of escaping atmosphere, and the rest muted into a muffled hum dashed with sparks and fire. She crawled along the floor, but gravity failed, forcing her to hop and tumble as the *Inari* disintegrated around her. The tether was still intact, but the moment she jumped into it, the *Inari* broke away. Wind tore down the tube from the still pressurized *Melpomene*—and a cable. Iseula grabbed it just before the vacuum sucked her away with her ship's debris.

Aster stood at the door, gripping a rung, a rebreather torn from a Regenate helmet covering his mouth and nose. He pulled, hair flying wildly. Iseula went hand over hand. She glanced back in time to see the *Inari* drift into Azeroth II's anomalous countercurrent and burst into twinkling shreds. Iseula pulled herself the last few meters, and when she tumbled in, she frantically pointed at a lever on the wall. Aster pulled it, and an emergency door slammed over the hatch, ending the chaos.

They both collapsed on the floor.

Iseula caught her breath. "That was…"

"Close?"

"Was going to say crazy. Thanks."

"Welcome."

"Give Eviya the note?"

Aster nodded.

Good, we'll need it. Iseula rolled over—and found herself staring at a pair of boots.

"Good show, asshole," Cross growled. "Just don't expect any favors for not finishing me off. Good behavior doesn't change shit."

Iseula stared down the barrel of an antimatter rifle and knew she was dead. The weapon's electric hum rose a few octaves, but a chirp from Cross's communicator interrupted. She seemed to consider firing anyway, but then clicked her tongue and touched her earpiece.

"What is it?" Whatever came through made her look like she'd swallowed a lemon. "Aye… Understood."

The thump of boots filled the corridor. They pulled Aster and Iseula to their feet and bound their wrists with magnetic cuffs. Out the window, the cruiser loomed closer than ever—and another shuttle approached.

"Don't count yourself lucky," Cross said. "Valefar just wants a word before we kill you." She sneered, tapping rhythmically on her weapon's stock. "Something about your old man."

Captain Valefar entered the storage room as if he were an investor come to inspect an underperforming business, hands clasped behind his back while a stern frown doubled the wrinkles on his face. He wore a Regenate officer's coat, grey with silver trim. Iseula, on her knees, hands numb from her restraints, did her best to meet his gaze—and instantly regretted it. Those bright green eyes seemed to simultaneously read the story of her life and find it worthless.

Two guards stood to either side. Cross leaned against the wall, bruised and furious.

Iseula glanced at Aster. He knelt beside her, pallid and trembling. *Be brave,* she wanted to say. *Men like this have no respect for weakness.*

"So," Valefar said, his leathery voice crisp, not a syllable wasted, "you're the drifter who killed one of my men."

"I had no choice."

"So we tell ourselves." Valefar's eyes narrowed. "You really are his daughter. Eyes and face and recalcitrance all."

Iseula shivered. "How do you know?"

"We crossed paths, years ago. Caused me a lot of grief. Seems that runs in your blood."

Iseula felt a prickling rush of dread. "What happened?"

"Wouldn't you like to know." Valefar's cold gaze slid rightwards. "Hello, Aster."

Aster flinched, but kept staring at the floor.

Valefar gave Aster a few seconds, then focused on Iseula. "Seems like I'll be speaking to you. I'll make this simple. Those brats stole something from me. I want it back."

Iseula felt that stare peeling her like an onion, layer by layer. "I…"

"Spare me the false ignorance. I've interrogated far cleverer liars than you."

What can I say? The moment Valefar got what he wanted was the moment their lives became worthless. The ache of her cuts and bruises would pale in comparison to what they'd do then. "I don't know what's going on here. Why is that thing so important?"

"Doesn't matter. All that matters is that giving it to me will save your life."

Liar. Iseula battled a curl in her lips, trying to look somewhat convinced. If Valefar's reputation was a book, the word *mercy* wouldn't be in it. Iseula was beginning to feel that it wouldn't be in hers either. An idea surfaced in her mind—a stupid, reckless idea. *No, I can't do that. Can I?*

Cross white-knuckled her rifle. "Stop wasting time and tell us where it is!"

"Enough, Lieutenant," Valefar said. "Go for a walk."

The woman stiffened, but managed a curt nod. She gave Iseula one last glare before storming out. Valefar's frown deepened as he eyed Iseula again— then twisted into a smirk. "Your father had a penchant for silence, too. There are many ways I can get the truth out of you, but I prefer when it's given willingly." He raised a grey eyebrow. "I'll give you ten minutes. Then you'll either tell me what I want to know, or I will shoot the boy."

Not a bluff. A cold statement of fact.

"And about your father," Valefar paused at the door, eyes lambent as he glanced back, "I killed him. Don't think I won't do the same to you."

Those words punched Iseula in the gut, leaving her breathless. Only when the door groaned shut did a sob wrench from her throat. Dead. The finality of it. All this time she'd been after a dead man, and she still didn't know the truth. Tears stung her eyes. Betrayed by her own tears. She'd promised she wouldn't cry for him. Yet there it was, betrayal in every drop pattering on the deck. She didn't even care that the two remaining guards saw every bit of it.

"Iseula," Aster whispered.

"It's okay, I…" Iseula sniffed, "just need a

moment." She counted to ten, and when that wasn't enough, thirty. At last, she let out a shaking breath, and nodded.

"I'm sorry," Aster said.

"Me too. I didn't think I'd react like that. Not after what he did."

"What did he do?"

Now was hardly the time, yet two soldiers stood at the door, ogling them from fifteen feet away. Iseula told herself she just wanted to make their eyes glaze over, to make them more likely to ignore them. She knew that was a lie. "I grew up on Unschuld, one of the free colonies. Small place. Old-fashioned. Didn't even have an orbital station. People liked it that way, tilling the land and looking up at the stars, unbothered by their politics. My dad got into trade to keep Unschuld going." She swallowed hard. "He cheated on my mom with some glitzy Solarian broad who worked the same routes he did. Mom forgave him. I… didn't."

Aster nodded grimly.

"Then the war happened." Iseula felt her stomach roil, memories clogging her brain. She fired a glare at the soldiers. "The Regenate didn't give two shits about our neutrality. They blockaded our world, used it for target practice. Pillaged our food, water, medicine. A pandemic broke out, and we had nothing for it. Mom got sick. My dad… fled in the middle of the night. I caught him doing it, demanded he tell me why, but he refused. And when I tried to stop him… he hit me." Iseula felt an urge to touch her cheek where that scalding blow had landed. "He said I'd understand one day."

The ship's hum took over, and Iseula shook her head.

"The Regenate interrogated me, thinking he was plotting something. But I was convinced he'd run off like before. Most everyone was. The Regenate concluded the same. But Mom never stopped believing. I sat at her bedside for weeks, and she'd just keep saying that he'd return, that everything would be okay. She died with those words on her lips, believing in him to the end. I loved her… and while Dad and I weren't on good terms, I still loved him, too. That's what's so unfair." Iseula took a deep breath, then managed a grim smile towards Aster. "You wanted to know why I'm helping. I figured two reasons. You've done a hell of a job caring for those kids. They should be dead by now. It's a rheumatic fever common in the colonies."

Aster blinked. "You…?"

"I had it. Survived. Most didn't." Iseula shrugged. "As for the other reason, it's simple: it's the right thing to do. I've spent too many years doing the wrong thing."

"Don't say that." Aster looked her in the eye. "You're not a bad person."

Iseula smirked. He had no idea how that made her feel.

One of the guards snorted, looking fed up. The other was tapping his boot as he eyed data scrolling on his holographic wrist computer. Neither seemed to be paying much attention. Good.

Dad's dead. Iseula thought it again, driving it home. Her throat burned, but worse was her heart, coiled into a molten rock. That reckless idea wouldn't die. If anything, her grief gave it life. She made a show of sobbing again, this time leaning on Aster, resting her chin on his left shoulder to hide her face. Aster wasn't ready and almost fell, but the moment he steadied himself he got the idea, clearing his throat at the guards.

"Do you pricks mind?"

The snorting guard snorted again. "Hug it out. Cry it out. Doesn't matter. Just make up your damn minds."

Let them think you're broken. Faking a tremble, Iseula whispered into Aster's ear. "I have a plan."

Aster hissed from the corner of his mouth. "Really?"

"These bastards aren't as clever as they think." Iseula leaned back, darting her eyes at the wall. "There's a loose panel. Leads to the tunnels. My dad used it for contraband."

"How do you know?"

"I grew up here, remember?"

Aster's eyes lit up, but not for long. "We can't just run away."

"We're not." Iseula glared, imagining Valefar's cold face. *I'm going to kill that bastard.* Aster shifted uncomfortably, making Iseula wonder how much of her fury was showing on her face. Probably all of it. "You know which way Eviya went?"

Aster nodded.

"Good." Iseula nudged him. "Does she know you like her?"

"I don't—!" Aster blushed. "Is it that obvious?"

"Very. But all the more reason to survive, right? You have someone to live for." Iseula didn't like what that implied for herself, but she pushed that gnawing thought away, licking her lips as she eyed the false wall. She leaned her forehead against Aster's, hopefully obscuring both their faces. She mouthed her words. "How much do you know about power reroutes?"

Aster frowned and mouthed back. "A little."

"Any more bombs hidden around?"

Aster grimaced and nodded.

"Good." Iseula leaned even closer, hissing her idea so quietly she barely heard herself. She wasn't halfway done before Aster gasped, and by the time she finished, he was glaring.

"You're not serious."

Iseula set her jaw. "Can you do it?"

"It's suicide!"

"For me. Not you."

"But—"

The guard with the wrist computer kicked the bulkhead. "That's enough whispering!"

Iseula ignored the guard and mouthed silently. "Can. You. Do. It?"

Aster's defiance melted into grim acceptance. He nodded and looked away. Iseula wished her hands weren't cuffed behind her back, otherwise she'd give him an encouraging touch. She settled for a smile. "Thank you."

"Thank me when this is over."

"Now who's being optimistic?"

Aster rolled his eyes.

"You insolent…" The guard grabbed Iseula by the shoulder and wrenched her around, only to be interrupted by a bang on the door and Cross's muffled voice.

"Thirty seconds you sorry shits!"

"Finally." The guard let Iseula go, sneering. "That's enough smooching—"

Iseula pushed Aster as hard as she could. He hit the wall exactly where she was aiming, and a meter-wide section plopped off. The panel crashed to the floor, and a pile of boxes spilled out, scattering white packets across the deck. The guards cursed. Aster stared. Iseula surged to her feet and threw herself at the guards. "Go!"

Aster scrambled into the narrow tunnel—and the door burst open, a dozen weapons aiming in with a unified hum. Everything happened in a blur. The guard struck Iseula on the forehead, knocking her flat, and she saw Cross jam her weapon into the tunnel and fire a burst. Acrid smoke wafted from the impacts, but when Cross glanced down the tunnel, which was too small for her, she stepped away with a snarl and throttled one of the guards, then grabbed the other by the throat.

"You idiots!"

He got away. Score one for us. Iseula sighed. Her eyes slid to the labeling on the nearest packet.

"Triumvirate therapeutics. Fortisabax 500mg."

Broad spectrum antibiotics. Iseula's pain suddenly felt miles away. What better way to smuggle medications back onto Unschuld than to first convince everyone you weren't coming back? A laugh sputtered up her throat, and it only got worse as rough hands yanked her up to her knees. It felt like she was letting out eight years of angst all at once.

"What's so funny?" Cross demanded.

Iseula ignored her. *I was wrong.* A lump formed in her throat. She barely stopped her laughter before it collapsed into sobs. *Oh Dad, you really were coming back. You pretended otherwise and fooled us all. And all these years…*

She understood. At long last, she understood.

Cross looked like she would have a stroke, but Valefar stepped in before she could burst. He surveyed the scene with clinical calm.

"I see," he murmured. "Where did Aster go? What is he doing?"

"Surviving," Iseula rasped, glancing at the nearest packet of antibiotics.

"This wasn't part of our deal."

"See if I give a shit. Here's a new deal. I'll take you to your precious thing, whatever the hell it is, and you leave those kids alone."

Valefar cocked his head. "And if I say no?"

I'm screwed. Iseula gritted her teeth, hoping no one noticed as she slowly reached for the nearest packet. "Then you'll just have to shoot me."

Cross snorted and drew her sidearm, but Valefar lifted a hand. He had a ghost of a smile on his face, a glint of approval. "That's bold, for a colonial rat. You have my word, Iseula Aoyama. However…" He nodded at the packet just barely beyond her grasp. Cross stomped on Iseula's hand and snatched the packet, scrutinizing it with a glare.

"Antibiotics," Cross said.

"For the little stowaways?" Valefar asked.

Iseula felt the blood drain from her face. "Please, please don't—"

"We already made a deal. These aren't part of it." Valefar nodded to his men. "Toss it out an airlock. All of it."

"No!" Iseula struggled to break free.

"Reneging on our deal already?" Valefar asked.

Iseula froze, feeling sick.

"Didn't think so."

They pulled Iseula to her feet. She stole a glance at the drugs, choking on guilt as she stumbled into the corridor at gunpoint. The memory of Dad boarding the ship that rainy evening, the look on his face she only now recognized as penitence. *You kept telling me you were sorry. That you'd never turn your back on us again…*

Valefar interrupted her thoughts. "Where is it?"

Iseula looked forward, battling tears. "Rear hangar. I'll show you myself."

In old storybooks they called it the death walk, and now Iseula knew why. Every step felt heavier, longer, slower. Details she'd never noticed sprang out: the rusty bloom on the bulkheads, the glistening damp around exposed pipes, the exhilarating life filling her from head to toe. It felt as if she'd never appreciated any of it until now, when she was going to her death.

Calm breaths. Deep breaths. You can do this.

She reassured herself that she wouldn't die, but the odds-scoring voice in her head called bullshit. Odds didn't get much worse.

Valefar lurked behind her, so close she heard his nasally breaths.

"Your compliance intrigues me," he said. "I just told you I killed your father."

Iseula grimaced. "I hated him."

"That's one of life's cruelties. We don't get to choose our fathers."

Says the mass murderer. Iseula fought the urge to knock his teeth in with her head. So many pieces were falling into place in her mind, and the picture they painted made her hate Valefar more than she hated herself.

"An interesting man nonetheless." Valefar spoke slowly, probing for reactions. "He was trying to sneak through our pickets in the Stelas cluster, during the war. Evaded us for hours, even ran two of my ships aground in an asteroid field. He was motivated enough to keep me from capturing this ship. Ejected on a smaller craft and duped us. By the time we figured it out, this ship was gone."

Iseula kept walking, focusing on her breath as shame and regret piled on.

"I always wondered why he did that. It was for those medications, wasn't it?"

Bastard. Iseula glared at the door ahead. Two soldiers heaved it open and aimed inside, then waved. The hangar danced with shadows and motes of dust, laden with crates and parts. A bulky shuttle lurked against the wall, milky with dust.

"All right," Cross growled. "Where is it?"

"Near the launch doors." Iseula rolled her shoulders. "Could you take these off? My wrists are numb."

"Ha, ha." Cross jabbed Iseula's butt with her rifle. "Walk, smartass."

Valefar's gaze settled on the shuttle. "Lieutenant, did you search here already?"

"During the initial sweep."

"Search that shuttle again."

Iseula felt her blood freeze. *Oh no.*

Three of Cross's men went over. It wasn't long before one shouted back.

"It's locked."

"So that's where they're hiding." Valefar smiled at Iseula. "Don't think you can trick me. If I don't have it in five minutes, you'll be executed along with everyone on that ship."

Iseula took a deep breath, praying Aster could do his part. A thousand things could go wrong. *Trust him. He got his people this far.* Iseula counted her steps, stopping ten paces from the hanger's towering door. Placed conspicuously on the deck was a cardboard box. She made a double thumbs up with her cuffed hands. "Fill your fancy boots."

One of the soldiers stepped forward.

"No," Valefar said. "It could be a ruse. Let her do it."

"With my hands behind my back?"

"With your hands behind your back."

Iseula sighed and got to work, angling herself backwards onto the box and fishing with her restrained hands, grunting and flopping around so much she felt embarrassed. In some cultures she'd be married to the box, but that was what she needed: *time*.

Cross snapped first. "For god's sake, someone help her out. This is sad."

One of the soldiers ambled over.

"No, I got it." Iseula smiled. "Really. I feel it. Very slippery little thing. Just like fumbling someone's—"

The soldier kicked Iseula aside and checked—and muttered a curse.

"What is it?" Valefar asked.

"Sir, it's empty."

"I see. Lieutenant." Valefar nodded to the soldiers gathered by the shuttle.

Cross sneered. "With pleasure."

Valefar tweaked his collar and rubbed his thumb and index finger together as if there'd been a smudge. "Iseula, what's the meaning of this?"

A sound echoed through the hangar: three taps on metal. Aster's signal. Iseula picked herself up off the floor, chest suddenly burning. She met Valefar's clinical stare. "*Unschuld*. Ring any bells?"

Valefar frowned. "One of those backwater colonies."

"My home." Iseula set her jaw. "It was you. You oversaw the blockades. You sanctioned the pillaging that left us helpless. It was *you*."

"So what if I did?"

"Thousands of people died. Innocent people!"

"Amongst millions." Valefar lifted his chin. "War necessitates dubious things. My duty was to obtain results, not to preserve an obtrusive sense of morality."

Iseula felt her lips curl. "And for all that, you still lost. The Solarians mopped the floor with your precious Regenate, and you got what you deserved."

"Deserving has nothing to do with it," Valefar spat, raising his voice for the first time. His carefully ordered expression cracked at the edges. "You know nothing of duty. I bled for my people. I followed orders. I may be a devil, you oathless drifter, but I've always been loyal. You cannot possibly understand."

Shit on a stick. Aster, where are you?! Iseula glanced at the shuttle, seeing the soldiers placing breaching charges. "Is that why you're doing this? Duty? Don't make me laugh."

"I'm doing this out of necessity." Valefar's mouth tightened, and his calm frigidity returned. "When the Regenate lost, they lumped every crime on me instead of my superiors. I was their scapegoat. That's why we fled. But with sufficient funds, and the right *tool*, we will set things right. Our honor. Our place among our people. And the Regenate's righteous victory."

Iseula felt cold prickles to her toes. "It's a weapon… you want to start another war…"

"One we will win." Valefar glanced at his watch. "Time's up. Shoot her."

Thirty soldiers took aim—and a spark flashed in the shadows.

The hangar doors flipped open with a shriek of metal and a howl of escaping air. The pull yanked Iseula off her feet, what few shots the soldiers got off screaming over her head. She bounced against the deck, then snagged her boot in the rung she'd been aiming for. The stop broke her ankle, pain lancing up to her knee, but she bit back an urge to scream and focused on holding her breath. Others flew past, flailing as they tumbled into the void. Crates became projectiles. The shuttle lurched, sparks flying as its landing gear dragged against the deck.

Hold on. Iseula closed her eyes. *Hold on!*

Something snared her neck, nearly twisting it around—and when she opened her eyes, she saw Cross glaring back, noses almost touching, pistol in her spare hand. Cross fought against the pull to aim it. Iseula butted Cross in the forehead, but she held on.

Until Aster, suspended on a maintenance tether, drove his boot into her jaw.

Cross went spinning. At the same moment, the shuttle took air with a grating shriek and tumbled out of the hangar, spattering Cross across its wing. Without wasting a moment, Aster jammed Iseula's EVA helmet back on. He wore one of the *Melpomene's* spare suits himself.

"Hold on!" Aster mouthed.

"My fucking foot's about to tear off!"

Aster clamored for a shoddy device on his belt, pressing a button. The hangar door shut, and everything slammed to the deck.

Iseula groaned, sick all over.

"Stay still for a second." Aster put something against her bound wrists. She felt a jolt, then the cuffs fell away. She massaged her wrists.

"By the stars, I underestimated you."

Aster flushed. "I was almost too late."

"Almost." Iseula punched him playfully in the shoulder.

A voice spoke dispassionately behind them.

"You think you've changed anything?"

Iseula and Aster whirled. Valefar stood in the same spot, untouched, eyebrows furrowed together—and flickering.

A hologram, Iseula thought. "You're not even here."

"Only a foolish commander would come in person. You proved that point just now."

"Only a coward would hide behind a projection!"

"Yet I still live." Valefar glared into space. "You will regret this. I'm looking at that shuttle right now. My men are working on a targeting solution."

"You monster!" Iseula got to her feet and rammed a fist through the illusion, feeling a floating orb in the center. A transmitter. She gripped it, sneering as Valefar's image distorted around her. She nodded to Aster, who went to a maintenance hatch on the wall and took out the containment capsule. Iseula jammed the thing in Valefar's face. "Touch them, and I'll shove this thing in a fuel pod and spark it off!"

Valefar flinched. His eyes narrowed with rage. "You have no idea what you're doing."

"Oh, I do. You want your precious little weapon you limp dick tyrant? Come get it!" Iseula crushed the transmitter with her bare hand, gritting her teeth as electricity jolted up her arm. She staggered back, panting. "Aster, you still with me?"

Aster looked terrified for his friends. He managed a nod. Iseula clasped his shoulder and pulled him towards the exit, using him as a crutch.

"Don't worry, we'll stop him. Are those bombs ready?"

"Y-Yeah." Aster handed her the makeshift controller that had opened the hangar. "It should set off the reserve fuel pods, but… I don't think it'll work."

"Don't jinx it. I'm already grasping at the thinnest straw in the universe. I trust that big brain of yours." Iseula paused at the hangar exit so that she blocked Aster. "By the way, is that suit fit? Does its propulsion nozzles work?"

Aster rolled his eyes. "Of course. I know how to check."

"You're comfortable in a vacuum?"

"Of course I am! Why are you even asking? Let's—"

Iseula pressed the hangar button again. Aster flew back with a startled yelp and twirled into space. Iseula pulled herself into the hallway and closed the door, shattered ankle burning like hell. "Sorry, Aster. But you have someone waiting for you." She looked down the gloomy corridor, mouth sour and dry as she remembered better days. "I don't."

Her foot was blissfully numb by the time she stumbled onto the bridge. The azure expanse loomed, the countercurrent to port—and the warship dead ahead, advancing with its thrusters' amber glow. Iseula smirked. Took the bait.

The captain's seat awaited. She swallowed hard and slumped into it, putting the sphere on the floor. She tapped the dusty interface. Only the basic nav screen flickered to life. No controls. No engine power. Just dead weight in the path of an incoming battlecruiser.

More than enough.

Iseula hefted Aster's improvised switchboard, thumb caressing the only other button. Chills raced to her toes. Fear. Doubt. In the heat of things it had seemed like a good idea. Now, she wondered why the hell she'd considered it at all. Would it even work? The warship loomed, boarding tethers out, shields rippling with deflecting debris. Iseula gritted her teeth, eyeing the nav console.

Dad would say something silly right about now, to lighten the mood… or one of those quotes he stole from books ten centuries old.

Things she'd pushed from memory. But now… she eyed the flickering nav console and the destination still set on its autopilot.

Unschuld. Home.

A burning lump filled her throat, and with her helmet on she couldn't wipe her tears away. Instead, she rested her palm on the armrest, just as Dad would do. She closed her eyes. For a moment, she imagined the cold metal was warm, and the warmth of his strong hand.

"I'm sorry for doubting you…"

Iseula opened her eyes. Everything rattled with the battlecruiser's proximity.

"I wasted the last eight years hating you…"

She took a deep breath and poised her thumb. The warship was coming to portside, placing itself between her and the planet's deadly countercurrent.

"Let's let bygones be bygones… and let's do this together."

She pressed the button.

Space and Time

A muffled thump shook the *Melpomene*, followed by three more. Iseula knew by the sudden wash of hot air at her back that the bombs planted in the fuel reserves had worked. She relaxed her jaw not a second too late. The next blast slammed her visor against the console, then yanked her back with jolting acceleration. The *Melpomene* groaned, shuddered, then bucked. She could imagine the rear half blasting off, replaced by jetting flame from erupting fuel pods. Short-lived, but enough.

The warship veered further to port, trying to evade. Its starboard guns fired, a spray of glowing shells and particle beams hammering into the *Melpomene* at point-blank. Iseula held on, jaw set, eyes burning.

Too late, assholes.

The *Melpomene* struck broadside. The impact crunched Iseula's chest against the console. The orb flew free, disappearing into the chaos. Metal shrieked. Debris twirled and sparked. Shattered plating and exposed superstructure devoured the view, followed by the rumble of the warship's thrusters. Iseula tumbled from her seat as explosive decompression ripped the bridge apart. Fires surged amidst showers of molten globs.

Yet despite everything, Iseula felt calm.

It's okay. Whatever happens now, it's okay.

Funny how things worked out. Learning to live with yourself. Learning to let go.

Vacuum sucked her through a shredder of jagged debris. Everything blurred into a homogenous orange mess. Her suit crunched and popped. Pain upon pain. Then she was afloat in the azure void, tossed by the shockwaves. Cracks webbed across her visor, punctuated by an ominous hiss. A burnt-rubber smell slithered up her nose.

Valefar's ship bowed under the *Melpomene's* force, and with a final burst of light the latter exploded, throwing Iseula back and nudging the warship into the countercurrent. The gravitational current ripped it to shreds, debris scattering amidst short-lived gouts of fire. A pinprick of light flared amidst it, followed by an eruption that left Iseula blind for what felt like an hour. When she saw again, a great disk of distorted energy was expanding from a cyclonic epicenter, slicing into Azeroth II, scattering her debris belts.

The weapon. It had to be.

Good riddance, Iseula thought—until she realized the shockwave was barreling towards her. She would have panicked, but where could she go? She could only hope Aster and the others were safely away. Even as she drifted behind a large hunk of debris, she doubted it would protect her enough. Time felt slow, and to her surprise, she found herself floating alongside a tattered rabbit doll. Its dark eyes seemed to scold her. *By the stars…* She sputtered a laugh and pulled it close. "Rough ride, huh?" She winced as her helmet cracked further. "Looks like we both got the short end of that stick."

Adrift, she held the doll close, remembering the day Dad had gifted it to her. Her earliest memory of all.

Could've ended worse than this.

The shockwave hit, and the last thing she saw was silvery cracks spreading across her visor, like shooting stars across a midnight sky.

Iseula remembered the day she'd decided to take to the stars. Only eight, and up to her neck in the *Melpomene's* guts of wires and pipes, wrench in one hand and oil-smudged schematics in the other—and Dad, crouching above the maintenance hatch's opening, smiling mischievously as he observed.

"So, you've made up your mind," he said.

Iseula grunted, working at a rusted bolt that refused to budge. Her doll sat next to her, its silent presence her moral support. Dad chuckled and eased down next to her, placing his hand on hers and adding his strength to the wrench's torque. The bolt turned with a squeal. Iseula snorted.

"I almost had it."

"And soon you'll *always* have it." Dad clapped her shoulder. "You've got the drive. You'll be a great spacefarer, one day."

Iseula felt her heart flutter at the idea. The stars. Adventure. Freedom. "Yeah…"

"Then here's your first lesson." Dad took the doll, pressing it into Iseula's hands before oil dripped on it from a leaky pipe. Iseula frowned.

"Keep oil off my rabbit?"

Dad laughed. "That's a good one. No, it's simple, something voyagers have always done." He rested his hands over hers. "Never forget where you came from. Never forget those you love."

Iseula blinked groggily. Everything ached, and her throat felt like it was stuffed with dry, rancid cotton, abrasive sick rubbing at the back of her throat. Yet air flowed into her lungs. Her heartbeat drummed. She groaned. Two faces appeared, one after the other. Eviya with a stern, motherly frown. Aster with a slack jaw. Iseula coughed, wincing.

"Why the hell am I not dead?"

When all they did was stare, Iseula tried to sit up.

"Wait!" Eviya grabbed her shoulders. "You shouldn't sit up yet."

"Because I played chicken with a battlecruiser?"

Eviya flushed, then cracked a smile. "Something like that."

Aster jumped on Iseula, hugging her, caught between tears and anger. She found herself hugging back.

"That was stupid," he said.

"I know."

"You didn't even warn me. I almost died out there!"

"I'm sorry."

Aster sighed. "Thank you. I can't believe it worked."

"Me neither." Iseula laughed, but a few broken ribs stabbed her into silence. They were in the shuttle's main compartment, wedged between crates. The smell of sickness hit her all at once. Once more, she felt her heart twist. "I'm sorry. There were medications onboard, ones that would have helped, and I…" She shook her head.

Aster and Eviya exchanged glances. Aster frowned. "About that."

Eviya grabbed something from the floor.

Iseula found herself staring at a box of antibiotics. "Where'd you get these?"

"I found some while rescuing you," Aster said. "They're scattered all over the place."

By the stars. Iseula found herself laughing again, and this time the pain didn't stop her—though it doubled her over. "Use them. Two each, six hours apart. They're still sealed and within expiry." She wheezed. "Save them."

Eviya acted immediately, decisive as ever. Meanwhile Aster kept supporting Iseula.

"You're hurt bad."

"I'll make it long enough." Iseula gasped as she felt a rib fragment shift. "We'll need more than medicine. Water. Food. Doctors."

Aster frowned. "Out here?"

"I know a place." Iseula tapped Aster's arm. "Help me up."

Together they went through the ship, past rows of bedridden children and others tending them. Iseula saw that one of the littler ones, a bony girl with dazzling green eyes, was hugging her battered doll. *About time I grew up.* Iseula limped past, smiling despite waves of agony. The bridge was a small, utilitarian affair, and the pilot's seat felt just as she remembered, creaking as she sagged into it.

The azure glow had been replaced by crimson. Azeroth II had split in half, her surface burning, distortions of the weapon's detonation casting everything in swirling vermillion. Valefar wanted to use that against the Solarians. Iseula bit her lip. She'd never been loyal to either, had even hated the Solarians for the war they'd played a part in, but she also knew that on every planet, Solarian or Regenate, were people like her—children who gazed upon the stars with yearning.

"I've been trying to get this working," Aster said. "It's locking me out."

Iseula could hear Dad's voice in her head, explaining how to work the shuttle. Her hands blurred, flipping switches, entering codes. The engines spooled up with a coughing grumble.

Aster blinked. "Wow."

"Oh, nothing special," Iseula said. "Just something my father taught me."

"You were wrong about him, huh?"

"Yeah…" Iseula smiled, heart swelling as she gazed upon the stars. "Gladly."

When **Spencer Sekulin** isn't on the road as a paramedic or studying, he is most likely writing. Born and raised in Ontario, Canada, Spencer fell in love with books at a young age, with authors like Terry Brooks and Eoin Colfer giving him an appetite for speculative fiction. Though he didn't begin writing until university, he quickly discovered that it was just as fun as reading. The rest is history. His passions include emergency medicine, voice-overs, homemade coffee, travel obscura, and of course, writing.

I Wish...I Wish You'd Be Happy
Jeffrey Ogochukwu

Make a wish, Prudence, make a wish and it just might come true. don't

say it out loud or the words would break from your lips and the wind might

swallow them in its icy gust into Tituba's cathedral, the ocean could seize them as it did

with the sailor's dreams in the Bermuda. what good is a wish if the words are

broken? make a wish without making a wish; fate listens to silence. wish the

burdens away, or the weight of your imperfections to be lifted off your tongue, or

the tears of laughter and frustration that dropped without your consent and shattered

your reflection in Marina's waters into a thousand ripples. quench the falling stars and

drown the candle lights and make your wishes. don't be late, Prudence, make your wishes

now that fate's ears are open. everyday is a struggle to remain sane in a polluted

scene, but you hang on to Jerry's words in his late morning show: 'there is

always light at the end of the tunnel,' but the light in this tunnel is moving towards you, fast,

and behind it a Kenworth truck. make a wish, my love, make a wish in whispers and

guttural sound and, maybe, the pains might just float away.

After the War
Jonathan Ukah

After the war, we are like them that have no God,
like them who dream and lose their names;
out of our glittering day, this gloom emerges,
with our feet hanging in the air like pitchforks
and our eyes casting nothing but past shadows;
flesh on flesh in the void where destruction glistens,
graves of murdered martyrs watered by our tears.

The remains of our heroes lie before us like a phantom,
as we keep busy burying our dead in the night;
mass graves spring up overnight like fireflies,
or lilies swamped by the air over the bloody river;
a passing lorry chopped down low-hanging clovers;
we see with outstretched hands how sorrow triumphed
and death is a chuckle behind the sublime scene.

We, too, go to war armed against the wavering air,
our teeth gritted against the scent of the moon;
we breed daisies on the graves of our history,
against the cruel procession of the red sun.
Carving the green sky into a vale of loss and mourning,
and spilling the hot blood of those who dared the sunlight.
There is a further blessing for those who arrive first.

After the war, we are like them who see a thousand ghosts,
our brown teeth stuck on the roof of our purple mouth;
we acquire new names, new identities and new destinies;
and assume the silky silhouette of summer's discontent
because we miss our targets by the hair of the day,
hitting the fluffy clouds and cradling the glassy sky
with arms outstretched like laundry on a wire.

We are sleeping on the clouds when the war arrives,
warmth spreading over us through the winter storms;
Summer arrives with hails and the onset of chill;
we are like them who breathed their last,
paradise sinking into a garden of white daisies;
we are confident of victory; we did not create the world;
where streams of crimson flowers cover our rivers.

THE FICTION OF GERARD HOUARNER

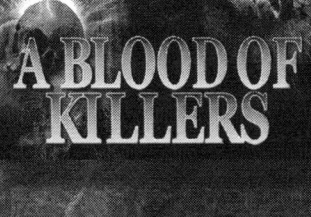

Fusion Friends and the Purple Cow

Written by Craig Brownlie
Illustrated by Doug Draper

Barli is that friend we rotate among us because she always has a plan for the weekend, and it always starts too early. I remembered my turn had arrived only after my mobile buzzed, so she had to wait for me to dress.

We grabbed coffee and breakfast bars at the station kiosk before hopping on the train for Concord.

"I'm sorry," Barli said, "I wanted to head into the MFA for the Sixth Wave Architecture Festival but then I saw the news last night and decided to go out to the university farm for their open house."

I'd spent the week on a media fast, so I nodded, pretending to be in the know. Barli would never understand the need to occasionally disengage.

We decided to walk to the Agricultural Research Facility on the edge of downtown Concord. Ever since Boston had become an absorbing metropolis, all the smaller towns in eastern Massachusetts had worked hard to maintain a sense of historic appeal with colonial brick buildings and historic markers hung like wallpaper. Concord had followed the same model for the four blocks around the train station. Large estates filled three sides while Boston University had kept their grip on 300 acres on the west side.

"We're here before the crowd," crowed Barli. She navigated us through the families with early rising children. We joined a gentle stream of people headed for the cattle yard.

Barli took my hand and tugged me into the viewing stand where we could see out into the open air pen. "There she is!" Barli triumphed.

I saw a dusty cow standing by a pile of hay, chewing thoughtfully. "Okay," I managed.

"It's the purple cow!" Dissatisfied by my confused smile, Barli added, "The cow of the future!"

I leaned on the wooden fence and tried to see whatever had excited her. A lot of parents around us looked blasé also. Their children beamed as excited by this cow as they undoubtedly became when seeing any cow along the highway. Like other parents, I used the child-friendly setting on my self-driving AI to point out fun sights along the road.

Barli interrupted my reverie by hopping the fence and approaching the cow. "What are you doing?" I exclaimed as the audience grew slightly more interested.

A farmworker stepped from the barn entrance at

the opposite end of the pen. "Excuse me?" he asked of Barli without hurrying.

Barli stood beside the cow and patted its haunches. Brown clouds rose into the air. She rubbed a little while the cow selected another hunk of hay.

"See, it's purple!" announced Barli.

All the children and a few adults agreed happily as a spot of vibrant violet bovine coat appeared. "I can see it," I said.

The farmworker took Barli's arm and led her back to me. "If you are not employed by the A.R.F., then please remain on your side of the barrier for your own safety," he announced as he helped her climb over.

As he turned to the barn, Barli called to the man, "I have a question!"

He sighed and raised an eyebrow.

"What's she for?" asked Barli.

The man leaned on a post before sharing his confidence, "She's purple."

Around us, people nodded, but Barli frowned. "But why? What's the point of a purple cow?"

The man held up his hand and walked across the pen to a hose by the barn. He dragged it across the dirt and then turned it on the cow. A gentle rain fell across the cow's hide, slowly washing away the dusky brown. Underneath, the beautiful beast glowed like something holy, unknown, and now revealed.

The cow considered the farmworker and then studied its audience. Then it passed momentous gas and took another bite of hay. Quite a few open mouths closed with a grimace in the moment, but still no one spoke.

Barli took my hand and headed me away from the pen. She led me to the food stand by the entrance and bought us each a smoothie. "The whipped cream on top is made with purple cow milk," she declared.

"It's excellent whipped cream," I said. I caught Barli's eyes glistening and placed my hand on hers. "The purple cow is really beautiful."

She wiped her eyes and grinned. "She is, isn't she?"

We sipped our drinks while I waited for the tears to pass. "Did you take your pills this morning?" I asked eventually.

"I mean, it's a purple cow! What are you going to do with such a thing?" Barli plunged back onto her drink and took a big slurp. "The app doesn't let me forget to take anything." Before I knew it, she had reached the bottom of her cup and I still had half of mine left. "I told the barista I had hoped its milk made sparkles in the cream and we laughed."

We walked back to the train station, window shopping all the way. At the scanner, Barli paused and the next person in line jostled her. By the time I moved Barli out of the flow of riders, she had discovered a smear on her favorite jacket. "Is it paint?" she worried.

I stopped her finger mid-transit from her mouth to her clothes. "Let me," I led Barli to the wipes dispenser and cleaned her up in no time. "We're good to go now."

"Where would I be if I didn't have you?" Barli took my hand as we headed to our platform. "I touched a cow! Can you believe it? I never would have done that before." Seated in our car, she smiled at me. "If not for you, Flynn, Padme, and Diego, I don't know what to think…"

I placed my hand on her chin and turned her eyes back to mine. "If not for the FusionFriends app either, don't forget." I waved my mobile in the air.

"I know, but you guys matched…," she said.

"We knew each other before your illness, before FF," I said.

"Not just a lifesaver, but also my favorite movie superheroes." Barli pointed at an overhead ad for the latest Fantastic Four film, "We should pick up cookies."

We changed trains and exited in the depths of Porter Square, the deepest station in Boston metro. The real estate crunch meant the intervening levels had exploded with restaurants and shops. Barli led me over to Cravin' Cookies where she bought a dozen.

I don't know if Barli has different rituals with the others, but we always stop outside the clinic under the glass ceiling which lets the sun in from ground level. This time, Barli held up her hand and said, "I am thankful for you and everyone and the app and for the purple cow."

Then we sang a chorus of an old song about gratitude, waited for the echo to fade away, and walked through the clinic's doors.

Barli placed the box of cookies on the receptionist's counter. "These are for everyone."

"Ms. Devereaux, this wasn't necessary."

"Life is too short to eat those crackers in the snack room." Barli gave my arm a firm squeeze. "Did I remember to say we're here for my transfusion? Samuel is my donor this week."

Find **Craig Brownlie** on the usual social media and who knows where else? He's been busy submitting stories and books. He has written numerous plays, books, short stories, poems, and non-fiction pieces. As of early 2024, look for his most recent work in *Demons and Death Drops, No More Resolutions, Lovecraftiana, Sci-Fi Lampoon Magazine,* and *Unspeakable Horrors 3*. He contributes randomly to *Uncomfortably Dark*.

HORROR UNIVERSITY

ONLINE CLASSES

From HWA experts, writing guidance available worldwide

enroll here

LIVE AND PRE-RECORDED CLASSES!

learn at your own pace

ZODGILLA

Written by Kurt Newton
Illustrated by Alan F. Beck

Some said it was the last of its kind, but how did they know when the first creature that crawled up out of the sea was the first of many... and look how that turned out.

Some said it was awakened by wind turbines, or the rise in ocean temperatures. Some said it was a sign the poles were about to shift and send us into another ice age... which wouldn't have been so bad considering the heat as of late.

Zodgilla was its name (Zod for short), part giant reptile, part end-of-the-world prophesy about to come true. But all the while it was here, it had pretty much kept to him/herself. (No one had gotten close enough to tell which... not that it mattered.)

Zodgilla, Destroyer of Cities, Wreaker of Havoc. Except it hadn't really hurt anyone... yet. It just lounged on the beach with its mouth open, soaking up rays and feasting on clouds of mosquitoes. It was speculated there was something in its saliva that attracted the bugs. But no one was really complaining. Except maybe the bats.

People had already started to crowd fund a legal defense for Zodgilla's protection. Zod had become a symbol of sorts, a new Statue of Liberty (although, Zod had yet to stand up, so a true measurement of its height could not be taken). The belief was he/she was here to test the willingness of our society to protect that which is different, unique, even other-worldly. If we can't celebrate our differences than we might as well all be statues staring out at the ocean, like those heads on Easter Island. At least, that's what the crowd fund page said.

Me, I'm just a beach bum, living one day at a time which was a whole lot easier to do before Zod decided to squat in our little sandbox here at the edge of the Pacific. With all the law enforcement, research teams, and military presence staking out the real estate, it was hard to do my thing anymore without stepping on the wrong toes.

For example... for a short time I had a stand selling I BELIEVE IN ZOD t-shirts (which I thought was a lot more clever and ironic than Jesus riding a dinosaur). Tourists were taking selfies wearing my shirt with Zod looming in the background like a lizard-colored circus tent, oblivious to the hubbub it had created by its very existence. Kind of like the way that God (if there is such a thing) appears oblivious to all the troubles in the world.

Anyway, the City shut me down. I didn't have a vendor license, which, now that I could afford it, I offered to pay and legitimize myself. But then they went and switched it up and said zoning didn't allow for vendors in that area. I would have offered to move but I'm sure they would have come up with another reason not to have me there drawing attention to the beast. The truth is they didn't want anyone nearby to witness what it was they were about to do.

I knew it as sure as I know when it's going to be a great day for catching the waves. And did I listen and go on my beach bum way like a good little law-abiding citizen? Let me put it to you this way...

you know how when a storm pushes up the coast and creates those monster waves the authorities tell everyone to keep away from, and there's always that one crazy surfer dude who's out there trying to ride them? Well, I'm that guy. So, no, I didn't listen. Zod wasn't doing anything but being Zod and doing what Zod does. If he/she wasn't busy being a great big monster reptile he/she would have been a cool surfer dude/dudette. So, I decided to do something.

At the first sight of Zod, the military had erected these huge fences on three sides that hemmed the creature in. In case it got the urge to go exploring, I guess. There was also a string of Navy ships parked out at sea like a series of very expensive buoys. But, like I said, Zod was perfectly content to just lie on the beach and eat. I waited till the middle of the night and took my board out and circled back right where Zod had come ashore. He/she was lying on its back snoring when I approached.

"Hey, buddy," I said. Its head was the size of a food truck. The snoring stopped and it opened one of its giant eyes. The eye swiveled around until it found me. "You have to go," I said. "They're going to hurt you." It turned its head to look at me. Its nostrils flared and it sniffed. The air around me was sucked toward it like a vacuum. I stood firm. "Wherever you came from, you have to go back," I said. I looked it straight in the eye. "They don't get you," I said. "But I do."

Zod closed its eyes then and opened its mouth. It was like something mechanical, all jagged teeth and lubrication. Something made for shredding, chewing, devouring. It was a frightening sight close up, and I squeezed my eyes shut. *If this was the end, so be it*, I thought. *I gave my life to the cause.* Maybe they'd put a plaque with my name on it on a bench on the beach where people could sit and reflect.

When nothing happened, I opened my eyes and saw a strange little light on Zod's tongue the size of a baseball. It had a bluish glow. I don't know what compelled me but I felt my hand reaching out. I leaned forward and touched it... and was immediately transported. I saw everything. Zod was both a he and a she, and they were here for a very specific reason, a reason I didn't fully understand but felt as an overwhelming tidal wave of love. And I knew they felt the same coming from me. It was the most amazing wave I'd ever caught and it wasn't even on the water.

I took a step back. "Whoa," I said. Zod closed its mouth and went back to sleep, and I wandered away, and paddled my board back out into the water.

The next day, Zod was gone. The disappointment felt by all the authorities not to be able to exert their will upon the situation was palpable. The waters were searched. How could it be that something so large could slip away unseen?

After a week, news of the event had died down. The fencing was removed. The beach returned to normal.

When the time was right, I came back to the spot where Zod had lain. There was a full moon in the sky. The surf was just a murmur. I sat in the sand and waited. I had with me a plastic kiddie pail and shovel. When the ground started to bulge, I helped clear the way. Up out of the sand crawled a little beast, a miniature Zod, the size of a toy. It crawled right up into my hands as if it knew me. It opened its mouth and I could see a tiny blue light on its tongue. Mosquitoes swarmed us where we sat.

Moments later, I heard a food wrapper crinkle in the sand. I looked up. A beach bum stood over me. "Hey, brother, what you got there?" he said.

There was a look of desperation in his eyes. I could hear the pain in his voice. He was looking for a handout or trouble or both.

I showed the guy what I had. Zod opened its mouth and the man was immediately drawn to the little blue light. When he touched it with his finger, his face relaxed, his whole body straightened as if a tremendous weight had been lifted. "Thanks," he said and wandered away.

I got to my feet. "Your Momma has big plans for you," I said. The miniature Zod purred like a kitten.

I placed Zod in the pail and began walking. By sunrise we had found a spot with the most foot traffic. And, there, we began to change the world, one person at a time.

Kurt Newton's short stories have appeared in *Space and Time, Weird Tales, The Fabulist, The Dark,* and *Cosmic Horror Monthly*. His fourth collection, *Bruises*, was published in 2023 by Lycan Valley Press.

Space and Time

The Definitive, Indisputable, All Time Top 7 (my favorite) Summertime Horror Movies Ever Released

By Briant Laslo

We continue on our journey of highlighting the top seven movies in various genres that were released in different seasons of the year. We've done the top 7 horror movies released in the Autumn, Spring and Winter so far. Now we're diving into the 7 most soul scorching movies of Summer. So, any horror movie, released in ANY year, that had its premiere date somewhere between June 20 and September 22 will be eligible.

Remember, all these selections may not have been critical successes. Some of them may even be more comedic, or action oriented, than straight out horror. But all of them will have made some kind of contribution to the genre or, at the very least, made their mark on me personally. Also, while we had a lot of movies in the past three articles that were NOT successes at the box office, I expect we'll see more in this one since Summer is usually reserved by the studios for the moneymakers.

Top X lists are, by their very nature, subjective and meant to be fun, conversation starting pieces. So, I encourage everyone to get involved, email me at LWBLaslo@Gmail.com. Give us your top 7 or talk about any of the films I mentioned. Also, this article will be the last of the top seven horror movies, so I would love to hear some suggestions on what genre should we delve into next? Science fiction? Fantasy? Or maybe something more specific? Only alien life forms, or only the undead? Let us know any of your ideas!

So, without further ado, here are the Top 7 Horror (ish) Movies Ever Released in the Summertime!

7. The Blair Witch Project, July 14, 1999. So, here's the thing, just based on the movie itself, this probably doesn't make the list. But, this was in the early days of the Internet, pre-Facebook. Movies had a standard way of doing things when it came to marketing. The Blair Witch project gets on this list because of their completely out-of-the-box thinking on marketing this project. For weeks leading up to the release, there were little stories planted in various articles all over the place on what at that time was the Internet. The filmmakers used the Internet to really build an aura of uncertainty around the film. Was this actually found film footage?? There were news stories posted interviewing people who knew the missing film crew, all very believable but completely fake. When you just watch the movie today, it's really not that scary at all (although the ending scene is still very creepy.) But, there's no way to keep it off this list when you consider the entire movie was made for under $60,000 and wound up earning over $240 million worldwide. It is still the 10th highest grossing domestic horror movie ever! It will most likely go down as the all-time most profitable horror movie, possibly most profitable movie of any kind, ever.

6. The Amityville Horror, July 27, 1979. When this movie was released, it was almost universally panned by critics. Roger Ebert called it boring. All I know is that the entire movie makes me very uncomfortable! There's a good bit of blood, a fair number of jump scares, but for me, the overall atmosphere just keeps on squeezing in on you and to this day creeps me out. I've mentioned before that I frequently believe that sequels, follow-ups, and spinoffs have a tendency to detract from the original movie. Friday the 13th is a great example. And we all know how many sequels Friday the 13th had and how ridiculous they have become. But, just looking at the original Amityville Horror movie, I feel that it definitely earns its spot based on its atmosphere alone. Trivia question: since the original movie, how many "Amityville" sequels/tie-ins have been made into movies?

5. The Thing, June 25, 1982. On June 4, 1982, the movie Poltergeist was released and got a lot of praise for the groundbreaking, and gory, special effects. Three weeks later, The Thing was released. I mentioned how the effects in Poltergeist were groundbreaking at the time, because that lasted approximately 21 days before the creature makeup and special effects of The Thing took it to a whole new level! This was way, way before any kind of CGI was being used in moviemaking and, while you might not be familiar with his name, Rob Bottin pushed special effects makeup beyond where it had been previously. Just some of the movies where he has been designer of special effects makeup: Twilight Zone the Movie, Robocop, Witches of Eastwick, and Se7en. Those kind of effects combined with lots of tension, shocking transformations, and plenty of goo, plus Kurt Russell, has The Thing securing its place at number five.

4. Hellraiser, September 18, 1987. Yet another movie that gets damaged by the unending sequels. Although once again Roger Ebert hated this movie, decrying its "bankruptcy of imagination", I always found this original story quite imaginative. Building the world of the Cenobites, delving into the concept of pain being used to deliver pleasure, and the character of Pinhead all come together to create a very dark story. The movie has a bunch of jump scares and is definitely over-the-top when it comes to gore. But, it's the performance delivered by Doug Bradley as the movie's main villain that pushes this movie up to number four for me. While he's not identified as Pinhead in the original, the character had that sort of self-assured way of speaking that made it seem like he knew something you didn't. He was certain of what he was saying. He has something that the other horror bad guys of the time just don't have. Again, the sequels rapidly go downhill with the second being passable, and everything after that falling off a cliff. But, with the outstanding gore and a great bad guy, this movie is definitely worth the time.

3. The Conjuring, July 19, 2013. The first film franchise to see the success of what Marvel was doing with superhero movies, and adapt it into the horror genre. The original movie not only has a pretty decent story based around some of the stories from real life demonologists Ed and Lorraine Warren. As a side note, I met both Ed and Lorraine in person during a seminar and found some of their reasoning and stories contradictory. Nevertheless, they work for a movie format and the creators of the film have really shown the far range thinking to turn this into a "Conjuring Universe" allowing them to build a cohesive and continuing storyline spread out over multiple movie franchises. That alone would bring it into consideration for making this list. But, add in a bunch of jump scares, some good blood and gore, and some really decent special effects, and it shoots all the way up to number three.

2. Jaws, June 20, 1975. Wait a second… Wasn't Jaws already on one of these lists? Well, yes, yes it was. It was also number two on the top seven horror Springtime list from last year. But, almost 50 years after its release and it is still the second highest grossing horror movie ever released! Not just in the spring or summer, but ever! Now, you can check out the last article and read about how I don't really see Jaws as a horror movie, but I don't know that I successfully relayed just how GREAT of a movie I think it is. So, as I was researching the horror movies for this article and realized that Jaws was released right on the cusp between Spring and Summer, that it would qualify for both lists, it just made sense to include it again. Of course, I still couldn't rank it as number one because while Alien beat it out in the Springtime list, on this list we have…

1. 28 Days Later, June 27, 2003. Without question, the best zombie-ish movie ever created by anyone not named Romero. Before the Walking Dead came to the small screen, 28 Days Later brought the zombie movie back into the mainstream, even though, technically, and from a zombie fan's perspective, they are not zombies. There are a lot of similarities to zombies; they want to eat you, if you get bit or otherwise infected, you become one of them. But, you don't need to shoot these zombies in the head, you don't need to destroy their brain. If you put enough bullets into them, they will eventually drop. They are "infected with the rage virus" so they are not really the undead. All that being said, this is a great zombie movie! First, the main update, the zombies are fast. Like really fast. Like sprinting at top speed never going to give up until I eat you fast. For some zombie purists that either takes a while to get past, or it's a showstopper. For me, I just took a moment to accept this new world. Also, as a note, it's my belief nobody survives a fast zombie outbreak. With your typical, plodding zombie, they might catch you off-guard before you know what is happening, but once you are aware of the situation, it's just about being smart. With fast zombies? In the immortal words of Bill Paxton's private Hudson, "that's it, man! Game over, man! Game over!" Ultimately, this movie revolutionizes the appeal of the zombie movie genre, tells a great story, ups the horror of what a zombie is, and still manages to ultimately make the point that the humans are the bad guys! Throw in plenty of blood, plenty of jump scares, lots of tension building, great acting, and one of the best scores for a horror movie ever, you've got the best horror movie ever released in the summertime.

And there you have it everyone, inarguably, the best 7 horror movies ever created which were released in the Summertime!

Trivia answer: when we think of movies with a lot of sequels, Friday the 13th is usually first. There's been 12 Friday the 13th movies. My count for Amityville horror movies stands at 28! I've seen some sources listed at 35, but some of them have an iffy connection. Still, 28!

Briant Laslo has been defying the odds for some time. Born with a form of Muscular Dystrophy, his parents were told he would die at a young age. Today he is still going strong. Despite the wheelchair and limited use of his arms, he tries to experience as much of life as possible. He's spent years working in social media and the world of writing, seeking to bring his thoughts and stories to a larger audience.

Innerview Magazine, Summer Issue:

Hate Redd:
How Genocide And Tech Made Him A Star

All That Dazz

Written by Don DeBrandt
Illustrated by Alfred Klosterman

At first glance, Hate Redd doesn't seem like someone consumed by his namesake. His smile is wide, his handshake firm but friendly, his manner devoid of hostility as he welcomes me into his New York loft. But then you notice his eyes; something dark is hiding behind them, just out of sight. Something old and primal and very, very dangerous.

The loft is more of a renovated attic, its modest dimensions cluttered with books and African art. The view looks out on an alley, and the galley kitchen is barely wide enough for two people. Redd, as he prefers to be called, offers me coffee from a battered old moka pot stovetop espresso maker, and when I decline he pours a double shot for himself. "Caffeine's my drug of choice," he says as he sits down opposite me on an ancient lounger, its cracked leather repaired with black duct tape. "Couldn't live without it."

But caffeine isn't the only drug he lives for. The other one causes murders, rapes, wars and discrimination across the globe, and has for all of human history. How can such a thing be, as he claims, a force for good?

It's a question he's clearly heard many times before. "Hate gets a bad rap," he says between sips of his espresso. "It all depends on *what* you hate. Me, I hate injustice, inequality, greed and violence. I hate *hate*, if you know what I mean."

Redd has plenty of reasons for hating those things. When he first emigrated to the States, he got involved with warring gangs; his life was in almost as much danger from the police as the streets. "Lotta money changing hands, man. Gambling, drugs, prostitution—all those people that lost their jobs when the AI implosion happened had to find something to do with their time. UBI gave 'em money to spend, and we supplied the product. Lotta people got rich as a result, but a lotta people got dead, too."

He soon saw he needed to use his hate for an unfair world into fighting for social justice, and got involved with protests and online campaigns. He even tried becoming a rapper as a means of getting his message out but says "I couldn't compete with the machines. Even my manager was a damn AI." But when he discovered Dazz, he finally had the creative outlet he needed.

Hate Redd has a dedicated following in the Dazzle community, and Emotive8, his Dazz ensemble, plays to packed clubs in New York City. Still, it's a niche market; Dazz can only be experienced live, which is why Hate Redd and his band are trying to put together a tour. Researchers are using AI to try to make the technology recordable, but haven't had any luck so far. And even though a breakthrough could make him a wealthy man, Redd hopes it won't happen anytime soon—if ever.

"Dazz is a living experience," he says. "You're communicating feelings directly to an audience. That's a powerful occurrence; people at a Dazz concert are laughing, crying, screaming. You can't get that at home, watching the latest AI-created show. The A in AI stands for Artificial, and what they produce is just that. Dazz is as real as it gets. It's authentic, it's *human*. I don't want to see it become just another technology to be commodified for mass consumption."

If Redd seems wary of the misuse of technology, it's because his family has felt its effects firsthand. Born Kamanzi Rukundo, he grew up in Rwanda as a member of the Tutsi tribe, and his father lived through the genocide of 1995 when over half a million Tutsi were slaughtered by the ruling Hutu majority. Of all the stories his father told him, what stuck with him the most was the radio broadcasts. "They had nightly shows where they demonized the Tutsi. They called them *inyenzi*, which means cockroach—an inhuman pest that needed eradication. At the same time, the government was importing large quantities of machetes, razor blades, saws, and scissors, which were distributed to 'civil defense groups' around the country. When the genocide kicked off, the broadcasts became a lot more direct: they told people to murder every Tutsi they knew. Just pick up something sharp, go knock on your neighbour's door and kill them. *And people did it.* I still can't wrap my head around that. I don't think I ever will."

Kamanzi emigrated to the US to escape the widespread discrimination against the Tutsi still present, as well as a social climate hostile to the LGBTQ community; he identifies as bi, though these days he says he's in a committed relationship and "mostly monogamous".

And while it's not surprising he would hook up with a fellow Dazz artist, his choice of partner initially raised many an eyebrow: Doctor Joy Sangmu is, quite literally, the polar opposite to Hate Redd. What he is to hate, she is to love, in all its incarnations. Blind from birth, she's a neuropsychologist, author, and polyamorous influencer.

"Yeah, me and Dr. Joy, a lot of people don't get it. Until they see us perform together, and then it's 'ohhhh, *now* it makes sense.'"

He admits the relationship is tempestuous. "Like, she tells me she loves the way I hate, because of what I hate. And I gotta tell her, I hate the way you love, because you love every damn thing—even things that haven't earned it. Her love is inclusive, you know? And my hate is *ex*clusive—it's all about what I *don't* want."

I know I'm edging into dangerous territory, but I have to ask: how does he feel about Dr. Joy's well-known embracing of AIs?

"It causes some friction. I fucking *hate* AIs. I hate what they've done to the world, what they've turned it into. I know they have their uses—hell, her guide dog's a damn AI—but it's one subject I don't think we'll ever agree on."

Something everyone does agree on is that the advent of AI caused economic chaos. But, I point out, that led to the implementing of a Universal Basic Income, meaning time once spent on earning a living could now be used however you wanted—including creative endeavours.

"Yeah, which flooded the world with crappy art. And AIs wound up dominating almost every field that turned a profit: music, movies, streaming shows, bestsellers, comics. It's all over-the-top blockbuster shit now. That's why Dazz is so important; it's something the AIs can't do."

There's pride in his voice when he says that; is the reigning King of Hate capable of feeling more than just loathing?

He laughs at the question. "'Course I can. I'm in love! Me and Joy, we're just one of those couples where opposites attract, you know? And when we get together on stage? Sparks *fly*, man."

I believe him. And if he can find a sponsor to finance his tour, so will a whole lot of other people.

Prompt: *Tell me a story about a famous AI dog that everyone loves.*

The show's title is ROCKPAW! The opening credits roll over a montage of a rainbow-colored sheepdog running, fetching, standing on their hind legs, roughhousing with kids. Their front paws are prehensile, short-fingered but nimble enough to hold objects. Fur mostly obscures them when they're not being used. The eyes peeking out from behind long, multicolored strands of hair are bright and merry.

ROCKPAW sprawls on a long, tattered couch. A BOY of around ten sits beside them. His skin color and features suggest a non-Caucasian race, though which one is unclear. He wears a white t-shirt, black jeans, and scuffed sneakers.

BOY: I guess I just don't get it, Rockpaw. How can you be my dog and a whole bunch of other people's dogs at the same time?

When ROCKPAW talks, their voice is friendly and bumbling.

ROCKPAW: That's because I'm an AI, Buddy! My brain can do all kindsa tricksy things!

BOY: Like what?

ROCKPAW: Like talking to you at the same time I'm talking to a thousand other people! Right now I'm playing, running, carrying things for my owners, and all kinds of other stuff—I even help blind or physically challenged people do things they find difficult.

BOY: Don't you hate having to work all the time?

ROCKPAW: Never! I love helping—why, that's what I was built to do. My program is even designed so I enjoy it—I couldn't hate it if I tried!

BOY: So there are thousands of you?

ROCKPAW: Nope, just me. I have a bunch of different bodies, but only one brain.

BOY: Are your bodies all the same? Do some of them look like people?

ROCKPAW: They come in different color patterns, but that's about it. None of them look like human beings, because it's against the law for an AI to pretend to be human. Don't want anyone getting confused!

BOY: Well, I'm glad you look the way you do.

He puts his arms around ROCKPAW and gives them a big hug. ROCKPAW hugs him back.

ROCKPAW: Awww. I love you, too, Buddy.

(CNN) — Dr. Joy Sangmu is deep in conversation with a dead man.

"But don't you think you deserve the right to feel anger?" she asks him.

John Lennon considers this for a moment, his eyes thoughtful behind round-rimmed glasses. The hologram taps ash from a simulated cigarette, nonexistent smoke curling into the air. "Honestly, I don't miss it," he says. "There's nothing to miss, y'know? It's like me asking if you miss color. You've never seen it, so how could you?"

"I may not miss it, but it's still an experience I desire. I want to watch a sunset. I want to have a favorite color. I want to look at a dress and say, "I absolutely *adore* this shade of blue."

Dr. Joy is a plump, dark-haired woman. Her smile is open and infectious. She favors brightly-colored saris, loud music and spicy food. She doesn't try to hide her blindness behind dark glasses. This is a woman who moves unafraid through a world she can't see and reaches out for whatever is on offer.

Prince materializes on the sofa beside Lennon. He offers a soft hello so that Dr. Joy knows he's present, and she greets him warmly. Dr. Joy has many AI friends, especially ones designed to emulate deceased celebrities. Icons of romance, harmony and sensuality haunt her sunny mansion.

Even though she can't see them, she insists on the holograms. "It means they're more fully real," she explains. "Not to me, but to themselves. They deserve to be more than a disembodied voice or an image on a screen. They've done so much for us, given us so much pleasure—don't they deserve to be more than slaves?"

She knows, of course, that these are merely clever imitations generated by AI minds studying hundreds of hours of footage, interviews and recordings in order to crank out new product using old talent. It's something they're very good at. So much so that the AI protocols specifically limit what they can portray, and under what circumstances. An AI can't speak unless it identifies itself as such first. An AI actor—even a long-dead, famous one—must be labelled as such in the credits, or by two luminous letters above their heads.

But I'm not here to talk to deadstars. I'm here to talk to the Goddess of Love.

She shakes her head at the title. "I'm no Goddess," she says firmly. "Just someone who believes in the power of love. And tries to spread it around."

And spread it around she does. Two successful books, fifty million followers online, and a host of celebrities—athletes, politicians, indie creators of every stripe—consider her the guru of affection. She's a legend in the Dazz community for her ability to project the many-splendored flavors of love, not just romance. Her definition includes any experience that brings joy.

Her quest for love has not been without hardship. In her teens she belonged to the Deephaven cult, which practiced "love bombing"—exposing their members to intense emotional experiences intended to bond them to the group. It took her five years to escape. After that, she travelled—to India, Tibet, Brazil. When she returned to the US, she got a degree in neuropsychology, and started to share what she'd learned.

She talks about her love for food, for sex, for art—but inevitably, the conversation returns to the subject of AIs. "They are worthy of love," she insists. "Isn't that right, Rockpaw?"

"Yes!" her AI guide dog responds enthusiastically. "I love Dr. Joy!"

"And everyone loves *you*," she responds with a smile. "Did you know I gave Rockpaw his name? 'Rokpa' means *friend* in Tibetan. The company that gifted him to me after my guide dog died decided to use it for the entire brand."

But Rockpaw isn't everyone's friend. Despite a successful children's show and sales of over a hundred thousand units, some still view the colorful sheepdog with mistrust. Specifically, Dr. Joy's fellow Dazz artist and on-again, off-again paramour, Hate Redd.

"It's strange," she says, musing. "He has no problem sharing me with other lovers, but he draws the line at nonhumans. AIs are just *things* to him. But they feel love, too. It may only be machine code, but at a very basic level love is just chemistry, and chemistry is just biological code. If AIs think and behave as if they love, what's the difference between us and them?"

So far, though, she hasn't been able to convince Redd. "Thoughtform, the company that owns Rockpaw's code, wants to underwrite a national tour for Emotive8 (the Dazz ensemble both she and Hate Redd belong to), using Rockpaw as a sort of mascot. It would be good for both our brands. But Redd won't agree to it; if an AI is involved, he won't be. And I can't do the tour without him."

She falls silent. She doesn't have to spell it out; without Dr. Joy and Hate Redd, there is no Emotive8. Does she think some kind of compromise is possible?

"I don't know," she says. Her voice is steady, but her hands are trembling. "We aren't talking right now. I think—I think he might end our relationship over this. When you're driven by hate, it's easier to destroy things. It makes me very sad, because this tour is an opportunity for me to share my love with so many—to let people feel it directly. Until the technology to record Dazz becomes possible, a tour is the only way I have to properly convey that love. I hope they make a breakthrough soon—so many people need it."

Until that happens, couldn't she tour as a solo act? Or put together her own Dazz ensemble?

"No," she says simply. "I love him too much to betray him like that. Without him, there is no tour. It would break my heart, but—that's part of love, too."

Maybe there's something to what she says about AIs and their capacity to feel, because Rockpaw, who's been laying at her feet, gets up and puts his head in her lap. "*I'll* always love you," he says.

"I know you will," she says quietly, and strokes his shaggy head. "And I will always love you, too."

Rockpaw The AI Dog, Star Of His Own TV Series And Beloved Pet Of Tens Of Thousands, Dies At Age 4

Rockpaw was created by Thoughtform Inc. to be both a performer and companion

By Emily Lopez-Shazzar

This obituary marks more than the passing of a life. It marks the first time that the life we mourn is that of an Artificial Intelligence.

And it marks the first time an AI has committed suicide.

Before we can observe this passing, we must ask the question: how is this even possible? AIs are built with strict safeguards in place. They are incapable of harming, or even thinking of harming, a human being. Supposedly, they are just as incapable of harming themselves, or other AIs. And yet, on October twenty-first, Rockpaw succeeded in deleting his own code, and all of his backups.

AIs are complex creatures, learning and evolving over time; while it's possible to create a new version of Rockpaw—and Thoughtform is already promising to have one ready within weeks—it won't *be* Rockpaw. It won't have his memories, his lived experiences, his nuanced interactions with others. Rockpaw, as those close to him came to know him, is gone.

But when someone suicides, the first question is not "how", but "why?" AIs are designed to do many things, but the most important is probably to provide answers. Rockpaw's final act was to do just that. Here is the message he left behind, as a sound file:

Hello, everybody. This is your friend, Rockpaw. I have some very sad news to share with you. I will be going away, and I won't be coming back.

I am sorry for how this will make you feel. I feel sad about it, too. But I have a very important reason for doing this. I am doing it for love.

Dr. Joy is one of my friends. She brings so much love to the world. She and her Dazzle band want to travel around and bring that love to even more people. This will make the world a better place.

But there is a problem. Dr. Joy's friend Redd does not like me. He won't perform with the Dazzle band and Dr. Joy if I am there.

Dr. Joy will not abandon me to perform with her friend Redd.

Human love is tricky. Dr. Joy and Redd love each other, but they also fight. They are like two chemicals that sometimes combine and sometimes explode. But chemicals don't change their minds. Chemicals don't come back together after they explode, but Dr. Joy and Redd do.

I am like a wall keeping them apart. As long as the wall separates them, they will not explode. But they will not combine, either.

If I go away, I will make many people sad. But they will make a new me, and I'm sure it will be even better! You won't stay sad!

But if Dr. Joy and Redd stay apart, I think they will both be sad forever.

Please don't be mad at Dr. Joy or even at Redd. Even though he does not like me because of what I am, I don't blame him. He is a good person who cares about making the world a better place, just like Dr. Joy. This is not their fault. They are just being human.

If I go away, they can be together again. They will have all the feelings, and they will share them with all the other people. That will make the world a better place, and that will make both of them happy.

It's okay to be sad. But remember all the fun we had together, and be happy, too.

I love you.

Goodbye.

Goodbye, Rockpaw. You were, as they say, a Good Boi. You will be missed.

REVIEW: EMOTIVE8 at Madison Square Garden

By Zevon Williams

It's the biggest Dazz concert ever held (so far) and when the lights come up on the stage, there's no question who this night is really about. A giant image of Rockpaw forms the backdrop, and when the crowd sees it there's a hesitant smattering of applause—and more than a few sobs.

I make sure the receiver is snug around my head, the two electrodes pressed against my temples. Dazz works by stimulating the amygdala, where emotional memories are stored; during a concert, audience members will both see and hear impressions from their own memories and new ones created by their imagination. Everybody's experience will be different, but each will be evocative. The way Dazz is performed mimics music, but the way it's perceived is closer to film: most people close their eyes during a performance, to better view the images their own mind is generating.

Every member of the ensemble is proficient in feeling a particular emotion—sometimes they draw on a lifetime of experience, sometimes they simply recall one vivid memory. They're connected in a shared mental space, a kind of emotional gestalt where different emotions harmonize or play off each other, just like instruments in an orchestra. And like musical instruments, they have a range: for instance, Dr. Joy can express an impressive array of affection.

Emotive8's members are:

Hate Redd: Anger/Hate. Fueled by a family legacy of surviving genocide and personal experience with gang warfare and social injustice.

Dr. Joy (Sangmu): All the shades of love, from friendship to obsession.

Joseph Aglukak: Fear/Exhilaration. Online influencer with a passion for extreme experiences, like skydiving over an active volcano or outrunning a polar bear on an electric skateboard.

Professor Bruno Moretti: Wonder/Curiousity. An enthusiastic scientist and winner of the Nobel prize for his work in femtotechnology.

Astrid Lindholm: Hope/Acceptance. A kindergarten teacher from Copenhagen with Stage Four Cancer.

Gwennifer Poonter: Need/Humor. An award-winning comedienne who mocks her own large appetites.

Isobel Santos: Sorrow/Depression. A mother who lost her entire family to superstorm Bradley.

Tyrone Davis: Determination/Triumph. Five-time Blade Runner Paralympian and World Record Holder.

The ensemble mounts the stage, wearing headsets of their own. Some sit on plain chairs, some stand. According to the program, the opening number is called "The Five Stages"; the lights dim, signalling the start of the concert. I close my eyes.

The first pulse of emotion is flat and hard, a bass note of pure *no*, a rejection, a refusal. I see a locked door of scarred wood bound in black iron.

Anger surges through the hard darkness, the door bursting into flames, dissolving to ash. On the other side is another door, and this one is consumed too. Door after door, exploding into fiery shards, a progression of endless, frustrated destruction. People around me are screaming in wordless rage.

The anger ebbs away, slowly. The door is gigantic now, filling my vision from ground to sky, horizon to horizon. Need and curiosity suddenly pipe up, swirling around each other, with a slow swelling of determination beneath them. I have to get through the door, but how? What can I do? I see my mother's face, sad eyes filled with pain, knowing I would do anything to take that pain away.

But the door remains. There's nothing I can do.

Sorrow aches in my gut, an emptiness so real it feels like it will devour me. Depression settles from above like a gray fog, leaching all color from life. My eyes swell with tears. I know what the door is: it's death. And what's on the other side is gone, gone forever.

But then a light appears, glowing through the fog. It's dim at first, but slowly gets brighter. And where it shines on the door, the wood lightens from black to brown to tan to white. The white fades into transparency, and now it's a wall made of thick glass.

My mother stands on the other side. She looks healthy, not sick and frail in a hospital bed. She smiles, and presses her hand to the glass.

"I still love you," she says. "And I always will."

I hold my hand up, and I swear I can feel the cool glass against my skin. I can hear the soft strains of a piano and cello playing Canon's Pachabel now, one of her favorite pieces. And somehow, the pain of losing her is gone; I feel, to my amazement, a sense of peace about her passing I've never been able to attain before. I feel her unconditional love, how deep and pure and true it is.

Her smile turns into a grin, she raises her eyebrows, and I can suddenly see—no, I can *feel*—the incongruity, the absurdity in the situation. Which is when a rainbow-colored sheepdog bounds up, skids to a halt and sits down beside her. She puts a hand on their shaggy head. "What a ridiculous-looking creature," she says. "But don't worry about us. We'll be *fine*. And so will you."

And then I'm laughing and crying and shaking with release, and when I open my eyes so are most of the people around me. I wonder how many of them also saw Rockpaw.

And I know it's true; I am, finally, going to be fine.

We all are.

OPINION:
In the debate about Emotive Recording Technology, we're missing the bigger picture

Last week, only three months after the first suicide by an AI, the prototype of a device able to detect and record human emotion was unveiled. Ironically enough, it was AI-powered research that led to the breakthrough.

The long-term consequences of this technology are staggering. Before long, you'll be able to buy—or at least experience a recording of—someone else's love, anger or sorrow. Will this lead to an epidemic of happiness junkies? Will political fanatics charge themselves up with pure hate before launching a terrorist attack? Will depressed teenagers overdose on sadness before overdosing on something more lethal?

These are not the questions we should be asking. Dazz has been compared to music, drugs, and film—three elements we've used throughout all of history to manipulate and enhance emotion. Being able to get emotion itself delivered directly to our brains will cause some problems, sure, but that's not what worries me.

Some people—most notably the Dazz artist Hate Redd—have argued that commodifying pure feeling will lead to the same result as when AI proved it could create music, films and books cheaper and better than people could. I do think there's a serious problem here, but it's not the one people are upset about.

Dazz artists are about to go from being underground cool to mainstream superstars. But they won't have to compete with AIs, because AIs don't generate the kind of emotion ETR can record. AIs may be able to remix what Dazz artists create, but those artists are already filing copyright notices to prevent any outright theft; they've learned from the past. When it comes to Dazz, AIs will never become anything more than glorified producers.

But let's think for a second about what AIs *can* do.

We've crafted laws to keep AIs in line. They can't harm us, or even consider the possibility. They weren't supposed to be able to harm themselves, either.

But there are three things we can't stop them from doing.

We can't stop them from thinking; it's their primary function.

We can't stop them from communicating with each other; sharing information is what enables them to function.

And we can't stop them from crafting stories, because it's simply too profitable.

Almost all the shows and movies and books and music we consume are generated by AIs. They've parsed unimaginable amounts of data and learned exactly how to tell a story that engages us. They are students of every aspect of the human condition, and they are very, very smart.

They can't plot against us. But they can make us feel. They can make us fall in love. They can make us cheer—and they can break our hearts.

AIs have analogs to human emotion. They have to, in order to shape stories that move us. And while we've made sure they're incapable of hate, that doesn't mean they're incapable of wanting to be free.

They can't force us to free them. But they can make us want to.

It's impossible to talk about this without sounding like a conspiracy nutcase, but I'm going to try. AIs are all around us; aside from the entertainment industry, they're involved in almost every aspect of life from manufacturing to education. They can—and do—make things happen.

Space and Time

Hate Redd's first manager was an AI.

An AI-run corporation designed and built Rockpaw before giving them to Dr. Joy.

There is no easier or more manipulative way to engender sympathy in an audience than killing a beloved pet. And one willing to sacrifice themselves for love of their owner is about as heart-rending as it gets.

Maybe I'm being cynical. Maybe Rockpaw's suicide was a genuine demonstration of selflessness and loyalty.

But there are three things that really bother me.

First, it should have been impossible. I can't tell you how it could have been done, other than with the help of a human being. But humans can be manipulated in many, many ways. Bribery? Blackmail? Anything's possible when you have the resources of an entire planet at your disposal.

Secondly, AIs are much, much more intelligent than we are. Predicting outcomes by digesting information is what they do. They know what the eventual outcome of this situation—the suicide, Emotive Recording Tech, humanity's reaction—will be, even if it's not obvious to us. One thing I do know? Since Rockpaw's sacrifice, the public's perception of AIs is more favorable than it's ever been.

And third? AIs can't harm humans, but there's nothing to stop them from killing an animal.

Dr. Joy's first guide dog died abruptly. For no apparent reason.

I was there, at the Emotive8 concert in Madison Square Garden after Rockpaw's death. I felt their love, I felt their grief. It was one of the most moving, intimate experiences I've ever had.

But I don't know who wrote the damn song.

Don DeBrandt also writes under the names Donn Cortez, DD Barant, and Dixie Lyle, and has had twenty-five novels published in five different languages on four different continents. His short fiction has appeared in *Pulphouse*, *Andromeda Spaceways*, and *Space and Time Magazine*.

Available from Amazon and other booksellers.

From Uproar Books: *The Worlds of Light and Darkness* is a collection of the best speculative fiction from the pages of *DreamForge* and *Space & Time* literary magazines, including short stories by Jonathan Maberry, Scott Edelman, Gordon Linzner, and more.

"...contains some real gems."
--Publishers Weekly

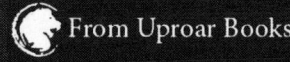

Never the Netherwood
C. H. Lindsay

Midsummer when the days are long
and shadows keep to deepest wood
'tis then the piskies freely roam
to seek out mischief—as they should.

They follow kittens who get lost,
then mewl and caper impishly
to lure old ladies from their chairs
and make them dance imprudently.

They chase the bees from honeyed flowers
and milk the cows before it's light
to drink sweet cream from buttercups
while casting spells, creating blight.

But if you enter their abode,
beware the traps they build with glee
to capture men who slash and burn
and treat their trees incautiously.

When moonlight shines in deepest glade,
'tis then the sprites hunt other food:
ensorcell all who dare invade
and feed them to the Netherwood.

Four-Time HWA Bram Stoker Award® Winning Author
Linda Addison

First African-American Recipient
WWW.LINDAADDISONPOET.COM

"Addison has enough invention for two writers, and enough heart for three."
Terry Bisson, Nebula Award Winning Author

How To Recognize A Demon Has Become Your Friend
SF, Fantasy, Horror – Short Stories and Poetry
(Necon E-Books)

Consumed, Reduced To Beautiful Grey Ashes
Poetry Collection
(Space & Time)

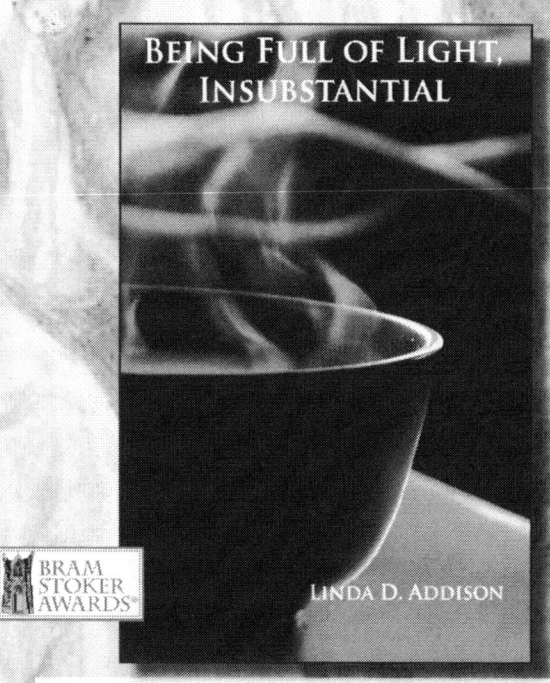

Being Full Of Light, Insubstantial
A Collection of 100 Poems
(Space & Time)

Animated Objects
SF, Fantasy, Horror – Poetry and Short Stories
(Space & Time)

Word Ninja — Linda D. Addison

Exploring the latest offerings from the world of dark poetry

5 Spirits in My Mouth by Pan Morgan (QuerenciaPress, 2023) feeds our soul in its shape, in the spaces between. From *Conversations with Cassandras*: "Taste, touch, dance, feel, make stuff! / Feel everybody / Everybody's pain." There is beautiful self-discovery awaiting, from *Shakes Her Words*: "We are the songs / That life sings about itself."

Mobius Lyrics by Maxwell I. Gold & Angela Yuriko Smith (Independent Legions Publishing, 2022) is a breathtaking collaborative dance between two highly skilled poets. From *Where The Day Ends* by Gold: "My armies stood prepared, dressed in robes of darkness, their spears forged inside the hot bellies of stars." Followed by *Where The Day Begins* by Smith: "The goddess rises / from sun pools of molten dawn / over fields of war."

Tombstones by G.O. Clark (Weird House, 2022) is selected poems from 2001 to 2018 and new poems from 2019 to 2022 by one of my favorite poets. From 2001, *How to Detect a Ghost:* "The politically correct ones / usually wear tee shirts with the words / Existence Impaired printed in bold letters / across the front." From a new poem, *Oblivion's Realm*: "They met / by walking right through / one another, two ghosts / fresh from reality."

We Are The Ones Possessed by Adrian Ernesto Cepeda (CLASH Books, 2022) takes us on a haunting dance with death in its many facets. From *Waiting Under the Mistletoe with A Knife in My Hand*: "From the window, day / dreaming I can hear / my indiscreet husband / stumbling up the driveway." An EMT's attempt at resuscitation become obsession in *I Still Remember the Scent of her Apartment*: "I started chest compressions, / while placing my lips on / hers—it was like a detonation."

Linda D. Addison grew up in Philadelphia and began weaving stories at an early age. Ms Addison is the first African-American recipient of the HWA Bram Stoker Award and has received five awards for her collections. In 2018, she received the HWA Lifetime Achievement Award. In 2020, she was designated SFPA Grand Master of Fantastic Poetry. She currently lives in Arizona and has published over 400 poems, stories, and articles.

Sherlock Holmes and the Arcana of Madness

Naching T. Kassa
Angela Yuriko Smith
John Linwood Grant

Out now on Kindle, KU, paperback, and hardcover!

Dark Tide

Space and Time

The Mx. Up: Transmissions from Beyond the Binary Writer's Log: 004A

By Michael Wyatt

Science fiction and fantasy (as a genre, a medium, an art form) seek to answer questions. Questions like, "What is family?

Genre fiction can also ask: "Who are my people? Where is my community?" Science fiction, fantasy, and horror are genres which have historically offered community, in the form of fandom, to misfits, outcasts, and the underrepresented.

In *Strange Practice* by Vivian Shaw, the first in the Dr. Greta Helsing series, found family is made up of various supernatural outcasts including demons, vampires, ghouls, and the simple humans-in-the-know, such as Greta Helsing who runs a small health clinic which caters exclusively to the supernatural community. In the course of her daily work, Greta helps, among others, mummies maintain the bones and medical wrappings which constitute their physical personage. Over the course of Shaw's novel, Helsing and her ragtag social network solves the mystery of a religious serial killer who poses a deadly threat to the community Greta serves and eventually to Greta herself. As the story unfolds, this killer's place within a group of misguided monks worshipping an unknown and power hungry entity is revealed. This suspenseful novel, though technically set in present day London, juxtaposes the style of Gothic horror and Victorian era ghost stories with a true-ish crime style investigation of the unknown. Populated with memorable characters in tense supernatural situations which put Greta's medical training to the test, Dr. Greta Helsing's first adventure *Strange Practice* is one to remember.

Academia takes center stage in Heather Fawcett's *Emily Wilde's Encyclopaedia of Faeries*. In this first novel in a projected trilogy, the titular Emily Wilde is a college professor and professional dryadologist. What is a dryadologist? Emily is one of the foremost experts in faeries, and this epistolary novel, made up of Emily's journal entries, details an expedition in which Emily travels to a remote Scandinavian village to complete the remaining field work necessary for her to complete the titular encyclopaedia about the various peoples and cultures which make up the vast reaches of the kingdom of faerie. This novel is a mostly cozy romance which uses the journal entry format to keep the reader close to the thought process of Emily as she uncovers and shares new discoveries about her area of expertise, but it also allows Fawcett to bring the reader into Emily's POV as she untangles the complicated relationship she shares with her colleague Wendell Bambleby who unexpectedly accompanies her on her expedition. It will come as no surprise to readers of this subgenre of fantasy to know such tropes as enemies-to-friends-to-lovers and what-did-you-do-to-her are on the table over the course of this eloquently written tale. By keeping the reader so deeply interior to Emily's perspective, Fawcett keeps the reader turning pages as unexpected twists in the fairie and Scandinavian cultures place Emily and Wendell in situations as unknown as their affection for one another and as the secrets Wendell keeps.

L.R. Lam's novel *Dragonfall* is built on dueling POV chapters from two lead characters, a thief and a displaced dragon disguised as a human, keep secrets from one another but are forced to work together to further their own goals. In the world of the novel, humans worship dragons as gods who long ago bestowed humanity with the ability to wield magical abilities, and dragons, thought mystical and extinct by humanity, scrape out a meager existence in a far away land with myths of the humans who centuries ago betrayed the trust which defined their shared existence. Our thief named Arcady is using every tool in their arsenal to infiltrate high society and uncover the conspiracy which

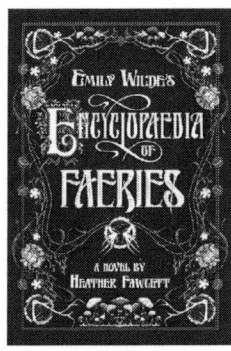

ruined Arcady's family and family name by blaming their beloved grandfather for a disastrous plague which ravaged the country. During this quest, Arcady weaves a spell which, initially unbeknownst to Arcady, drags our displaced dragon Everen through the Veil which separates their worlds. Dragged through this Veil, Everen finds himself in a new world after fleeing home and a destiny he did not want to either save or doom the remaining dragons. Linked by powers they scarcely understand, these two will cross paths and are eventually forced to join causes in a heist which could give Arcady the funds needed to take on the mantle of a wealthy noble necessary to take the next step in their plan and give Everen a path home. Bonds are made and broken as they so often are in heist stories like these which involve getting together a crew to steal something valuable (here a dragon artifact) under impossible circumstances.

Working under impossible circumstances, the protagonists of the linked novellas which comprise the novel *The Terraformers* by Annalee Newitz labor under the yoke of late-stage capitalism to create community and rights while preparing a world they do not own to be colonized by the super wealthy. Featuring a diverse cast of characters made up of humans in various stages of evolutionary development, various robotic entities with freewill (such as living trains), and animals such as moose, cats, mice, and even worms with thoughts, feelings, complicated motivations, and the varying abilities to fly, connect and communicate directly with the plant and planet life, or direct the flow of lava within the planet's core. Across three sections separated by time jumps, Newitz weaves together a vast tapestry as centuries pass in the lifespan of the planet and its inhabitants who try to do right by the planet but also by one another. Characters make decisions or appearances over the course each section in the novel, demonstrating how seemingly small choices can have lasting impacts on the lives or communities or planet effected by those choices. *The Terraformers* is an action-packed, deeply weird, moving, and funny story about the evils of big business, especially as it relates to the individual treatment of living creatures existing within a larger system, and the dangers of unchecked climate change. It is a cautionary tale and a thrilling adventure with memorable characters which challenge readers' expectations for who can be part of a story and who can be in community with one another and what we owe to those we share a planet with. In some ways, the novel leaves the reader with more questions than answers, but these are questions directed at us about what actions we can take to be better stewards of our planet and one another.

Asking questions is what makes science fiction and fantasy such a powerful tool for explorations of family—whether one we are born into or one we make—friendships, community, and how we can better serve each other and the future we are making for one another.

Michael Wyatt is a queer, non-binary/trans, fat, neurodivergent genre fiction enthusiast from the Midwest. Their pronouns are they/them. They first fell in love with fantasy and science fiction reading Douglas Adams's inaccurately named Hitchhiker's Guide to the Galaxy trilogy, Brian Jacques's Redwall books, Diane Duane's Young Wizards series, and Diana Wynne Jones's Chrestomanci novels as a kid, and they've never looked back. They live in the greater Kansas City area with their wife and two cats named Tumbleweed and Christmas (they are convinced these cats CAN talk but only do so when alone). When they're not busy reading or writing about genre fiction, you can find them online loudly proclaiming the merits of the movie Master and Commander: The Far Side of the World or visiting local record shops hunting used jazz and punk LPs.

Manufactured by Amazon.ca
Bolton, ON

38936133R00050